Emma in Buttonland

In memory of my grandmother, Lisbeth Heinzig,
whose button box inspired me even as a child to
write this story.   *UR*

In tribute to my grandparents from Vorarlberg.
                                    SL

Ulrike Rylance

Emma in Buttonland

Illustrated by Silke Leffler

Translated from German by Connie Stradling Morby

Sky Pony Press
New York

CONTENTS

NOTHING BUT PUZZLES

"Children," Uncle Hubert used to say, "should be seen and not heard." Then he would almost always let out a giddy laugh and add, "Naturally, it would be best if you didn't have to see them in the first place."

He was a small, fat man with a big mustache, which sat on his upper lip like a furry caterpillar.

Emma secretly thought that it would have been very pleasant not to have to see Uncle Hubert all the time either, but she didn't dare say that. After all, that wasn't very polite; and she was a little bit afraid of Uncle Hubert's false teeth. Because when her uncle was in a good mood (which was usually the case), or if he bad-mouthed children, sometimes in the heat of the moment his false teeth slipped out. Like a little living creature, they skipped over the table and then lay still somewhere, tipped over on their side. The yellowish teeth looked like the skeleton of a prehistoric fish. The dentures came from Uncle Hubert's father. Uncle Hubert would never throw out anything that could still be used.

Then Aunt Mechthild would always say, "Hubert, dear, your teeth."

After breakfast, once her uncle had his false teeth clamped firmly in his mouth, he and her aunt would likely start on a puzzle. All their love went to the puzzle pieces. Throughout the years they had put together countless numbers of puzzles, none of them under five thousand pieces. When they were finished with one, Uncle Hubert glued it on a board and hung it up somewhere or other.

It was very fortunate that they had such an enormous house. Uncle Hubert's father, the original owner of the false teeth, had been the

director of a tin can factory and had bought the twenty-five-room villa. With great foresight, as it turned out, since Uncle Hubert couldn't
throw out a thing; and with Aunt Mechthild putting together one
puzzle after another at breakneck speed, they would otherwise never
have had room for everything.

When Emma arrived at the villa a while ago, Aunt Mechthild
showed her all the rooms.

"The stone room, the snail shell room, the ticket room, the eye-
glasses room, the perfume sample room, the catalog room, the receipt
room, the stamp room, the ballpoint pen room . . . "

Aunt Mechthild briefly opened one door after another, so that the
bewildered Emma could just catch a glimpse of gigantic piles of snail
shells or ballpoint pens or mail order house catalogs before her aunt
closed them again, going at full tilt. "The button room," her aunt just
murmured, but didn't open the door. She looked almost anxious as
she said it.

"What are all of those things?" Emma asked, confused.

"Things that you find or get for free," her aunt explained.

"And what do you plan to do with them?"

Confronted with this question, Uncle Hubert turned fiery red. "She
asked what we plan to do with them? Keep them, of course! You
never know what might happen."

Emma thought over what might happen and on what occasion a
room full of receipts could possibly prove useful, but she was unable
to come to a reasonable conclusion. Her aunt and uncle were rather
quirky, but Emma didn't want to contradict them because of how
long she had to stay here—until her mother got back from
her trip to Africa. That meant until the end of summer vacation. She hoped that her mother would come back sooner.

Then they would both finally live at their house again, without puzzles and rooms full of garbage.

"Who'd like a surprise?" asked Uncle Hubert after breakfast one day.

"You don't possibly have . . . ?" asked her aunt, her cheeks red with eager anticipation.

"Yes, my dear, I do!" Her uncle rubbed his hands together and stomped his feet with excitement. "Twelve thousand pieces, special edition!" He pulled an enormous box from behind the couch. Aunt Mechthild clapped her hands.

"What kind of theme does the puzzle have?" she asked greedily.

Uncle Hubert made a dramatic pause.

"The Black Forrest!" he blurted out, unable to keep his surprise to himself any longer.

"The Black Forrest!" squeaked Aunt Mechthild with great enthusiasm.

Emma watched as the two of them tipped all the puzzle pieces onto the floor and tore into them like bloodhounds. Almost all the pieces looked the same and were either dark or light green. Aunt Mechthild's red hair shone like a campfire in the green jumble. Emma was more bored than she'd ever been in her whole life.

"I'm going to take a little walk," she said after a while.

"Children," said Uncle Hubert without looking up, "should be seen and not heard."

Emma scampered into the hall and, just as she closed the door behind her, a clacking noise sounded in the room.

"Hubert, dear, your teeth," she heard her aunt say.

Emma let out a deep sigh. Now what should she do?

THE SECRET ROOM

Emma roamed through the big house. When she passed the open kitchen door, she saw Mrs. Schulz, the plump cook. Mrs. Schulz was sitting on a chair, feet propped on a stool, sleeping with her mouth open. She was wearing weird rolled stockings on her legs, almost like a mummy. "Support stockings," she had explained to Emma. "To prevent varicose veins when you have to stand so much."

Emma didn't know what varicose veins were; besides, Mrs. Schulz seemed to take care of everything while sitting down anyway. Every so often she trudged, sighing, into the garden to get vegetables or herbs. In the process she always murmured, "What a burden it is, what a burden", as her mummy stockings rasped as she walked. It sounded like *krrrp, krrp, krrp*.

Emma decided not to wake Mrs. Schulz. What good would that do?

The cook was quite possibly a thousand times more boring than Uncle Hubert and Aunt Mechthild put together. In front of Mrs. Schulz was a bowl of luscious red apples. Pepper, the cook's gray cat, was lying next to her on the floor. He appeared to be sleeping, too, but as Emma came nearer so she could swipe an apple, he suddenly opened one eye and meowed.

Mrs. Schulz twitched her eyebrows restlessly and shifted her left leg over her right, making a little *krrrp* sound.

Emma decided to skip the apple and tiptoed back to the hall.

Next to her was the snail shell room. She opened the door and went in. It was deathly still inside and smelled a little musty, like in a museum. Some of the snail shells were very pretty to look at; others were broken or dingy. What was her uncle going to do with them? If only Emma had at least been allowed to use them for some crafts!

She picked up a little shell. There was something dry inside. She nearly dropped it. How disgusting.

Something behind her went "Meow." Pepper had followed her.

"Hey, Pepper," said Emma. "Do you feel like playing?"

Pepper just rubbed against her legs and ran out of the room. "Meow," he went again, and turned to look at her, almost as if he wanted to tell her something.

"What's the matter with you?" she wondered aloud, and followed him curiously. Pepper ran on lithe paws through the long hallway and stopped in front of a door.

"Meow!" He stood in front of the room that Aunt Mechthild had called the "button room," but whose door she hadn't opened.

"Yes, the button room. So what? Just more boring knickknacks," said Emma.

Pepper laughed.

Emma gaped at him in astonishment.

No, she thought, of course he didn't laugh; how could he have done that? After all, cats can't laugh. And yet it seemed to Emma that someone very close by was snickering quietly.

"Did you say something?" she asked Pepper suspiciously, feeling quite silly. Good thing that nobody could hear her.

Pepper certainly did not look at all cheerful—quite the opposite. He ran back and forth nervously in front of the door and kept scratching at the wood.

"You want to go in, is that it?" asked Emma again. "I'm not sure if we're allowed. Aunt Mechthild didn't say anything, but she didn't open this door either." She thought it over. Why was that?

In the meantime, Pepper was behaving like a crazy rubber ball. He flung himself with all his might against the door and yowled and meowed for all he was worth. There was a very clear rustling behind the door now.

Suddenly, Emma understood. There were mice inside! And Aunt Mechthild was terrified of them; that's why she hadn't opened the door.

Or was it . . . Emma's breath caught. Was it rats, maybe? But rats . . . did rats laugh? No, the idea was simply too ludicrous.

"Pepper," she said decisively. "There's only one way to find out."

Emma turned the doorknob.

The door was locked.

That was odd. All the other rooms in the house were open. Could her aunt be so deathly afraid of mice that she had locked the door? And where was the key?

It occurred to Emma that Mrs. Schulz owned a big key ring.

"You wait here!" she ordered Pepper, so that he didn't wake the cook with his yowling.

Mrs. Schulz was still sitting on her chair; now, there were little whistling sounds coming out of her mouth. The key ring was hanging on the belt of her apron. Carefully, Emma began to untie the bow. There was a soft jangling. Mrs. Schulz gasped for breath, murmured, "It's a burden, a miserable burden it is," and dozed off again.

Emma scampered back to the mysterious room and started trying the keys. The fourth one fit.

"Well, Pepper, here we go," she said, and opened the door.

Pepper shot into the room like a bolt of lightning, and although there was no light on, Emma could see something tiny dash over the floor. So it was mice!

"Eeew!" she squeaked, horrified. But wait, the crawling thing was too little to be a mouse; perhaps it was a spider?

Emma quickly hit the light switch on the wall with her hand. There was nothing more to be seen. Only countless boxes full of buttons. There must have been thousands, in all colors and sizes.

Without moving, Pepper, however, sat as though hypnotized in front of a corner cabinet and stared at something under it.

"Pepper, come here," scolded Emma. "There's nothing there!" She'd probably been mistaken; at any rate there were no spiders or mice here. When the cat didn't react, she lay down on her stomach and took a look for herself. "So, what's the matter?" She could see something gold twinkling under the cabinet. A coin? No, something else. She squinted. Then she recognized it.

"That's a button, you silly old cat. You can't eat that. Do you want to choke?"

Shaking her head, she pushed the animal aside. She looked around. The buttons were much more beautiful than the junk in the other rooms. It didn't smell so musty in here, either.

The cat was driving her crazy. He was acting like he was going to die if he didn't get the golden button under the cabinet right away! Again and again he stretched his paw toward it longingly. Emma lifted the fidgeting animal and put it down in front of the door in the hall.

"You wait here," she said firmly. "I want to look at the buttons in peace. And don't you dare wake Mrs. Schulz!"

Pepper looked mortally offended. Back in the button room, Emma closed the door behind her and took the box that was lying closest to her on a table. Inside, there were tiny buttons in all different colors. They were barely bigger than the nail on Emma's pinky. Some were shaped like little flowers.

Suddenly, she had an idea. She would play with the buttons! If there was no dollhouse here, at least she could play school with the tiny objects.

She sorted out a handful of little flower buttons. "You're the girls," she said. "And you," she reached into the box again, "are the boys." The boys were blue or gray or black. She placed all the students in a row.

Now all she needed was a teacher. The big gold button under the cabinet crossed her mind. It reminded her of her nice teacher at home, Mrs. Melzer. She liked to wear gold jewelry, too, and was a little chubby. Emma lay down on her stomach again and tried to grab the button, but without success.

"Well, come here," gasped Emma. "You're going to be the teacher! I'm going to call you Mrs. Melzer!"

Then something strange happened. The button ran away! It didn't roll; no, it ran on two tiny legs into the farthest corner under the cabinet where there were a bunch of dust bunnies.

What was going on here?

"Mrs. Melzer?" whispered Emma.

The button came back at once. To her amazement, she noticed that it also had two tiny arms and stood with its hands on its hips.

And then the unbelievable happened; the button began to talk!

"Those aren't students, you silly thing," said the golden button.

"Those are just plastic buttons! And I'm no teacher! And will you stop calling me Mrs. Melzer; what kind of a ridiculous name is that?"

Startled, Emma jumped and whammed her head on the cabinet.

"Ow, that must have hurt!" exclaimed the button.

"Wh, wh, what?" stammered Emma. "You can talk?" Carefully she extended her little finger toward the gold button.

"And speak to me politely," screeched the button. "I'm an aristocrat!"

"An aristocrat," repeated Emma, stunned. I'm talking with a button, she thought. Obviously, I've gone completely crazy. I've probably seen too many little puzzle pieces.

Or, was it some kind of magic?

Whatever it was, she had to have this talking button. It was the best thing she'd come across so far in this boring house. Longingly, she thrust her hand under the cabinet the way the cat had done before.

Her arm was longer than Pepper's. She stretched out her fingers.

Finally!

The moment she touched the button, a strange whirring noise began, as if a storm were sweeping through the room.

Suddenly it got dark.

LADY ISOLDE

Emma opened her eyes. All around her it was light again. Where was she? There were odd little houses here, painted in every color possible. Everything was so colorful! Even the road on which she was standing was bright blue with pretty white designs. The road seemed familiar, but the town was completely strange. And anyway—how could she be in a strange town when she had just crawled under the cabinet? Not far from her something sparkled in the sunlight. It was an unbelievably fat lady in a magnificent golden bubble dress.

"Hello?" Emma called tentatively.

The lady stared at her, but didn't answer. She wiped her face with a golden handkerchief. Even her skin had a metallic shimmer.

"Are you a neighbor of Aunt Mechthild's?" asked Emma.

The golden lady snorted with disdainful laughter.

"Neighbor? That'll be the day! I live alone! What kind of a button are you?"

"Button?" Emma blinked in confusion. What kind of a question was that?

"Button?" mimicked the lady. "Of course, button. What else? Earthworm maybe?" She chuckled as though it were a good joke, then took a step toward Emma.

"I'm not a button," answered Emma.

"Not a button? Not a button!" The lady dropped her handkerchief in shock.

"Are you a button?" asked Emma cautiously. When talking to lunatics, you always had to pretend to believe them, at least that was what she had heard.

"Address me politely!" bellowed the lady. "I'm an aristocrat! Lady Isolde is my name!"

All of a sudden Emma felt like somebody had opened a curtain. Of course—she was speaking with the button that had been under the cabinet! The button had claimed to be aristocratic too. There was no other explanation. Somehow, Emma had shrunk and was now having a conversation with the big, round, gold button.

"Where am I?" she asked, bewildered.

"Braid Street, see. What did you mean, you're not a button, hmm?"

The lady came closer and blinked with curiosity at Emma. There was something about her expression that Emma did not like at all.

Isolde bent forward. "Are you perhaps . . . " She became quiet, took a quick glance from right to left, and whispered, "Are you perhaps a stone?"

Emma shook her head. "Of course not. I'm a girl. My name is Emma."

Isolde looked at her, agape. Emma could see that even her eyes and eyelashes were golden.

"Ah!" Isolde's sudden cry was so loud that Emma reeled back in alarm and fell on her butt.

"Are you kidding me? A girl? Do you think that I've never seen a girl in my two hundred years? They're gigantic! Gigantic! Not as gigantic as their parents, but, nevertheless, not as tiny as you! I know exactly what you are. You're a stone. Or even worse, a cherry pit. Ugh, yuck. I'm going to report you!"

With that, Isolde gathered her bouffant skirt and scurried away with unexpected speed.

"Hey!" yelled Emma, frightened. Under no circumstances did she want to stay here alone. "I really was big once! Come back!"

"Be polite!" yelled Isolde without turning around. "That's: Come back, please, your ladyship!" Hastily, the button lady turned the corner at the end of the blue street and was gone.

Emma felt like crying. But at that moment she realized why she recognized the pattern on the road. Aunt Mechthild owned a skirt that had the very same blue braid sewn on the bottom edge.

She looked up. Right above her hung a beautifully decorated street sign. It looked crocheted. Braid Street, it read. That's exactly what Isolde had said. That meant . . .

That meant that this was the same braid, the one on Aunt Mechthild's skirt! The buttons had used it to build a road. She would continue along Braid Street and would surely get back to the button room soon.

And somehow she would also get big again.

That's what Emma hoped anyway.

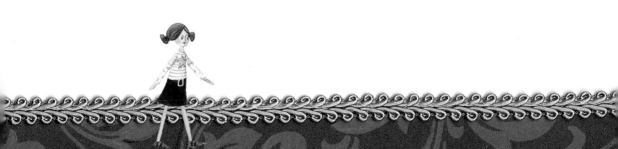

A CHILD, NOT A BUTTON

For a while Emma ran along the road. It was comfortably soft, like an expensive rug; there was no other way to describe it. Only now she noticed that the colorful houses on the edge of the road were apparently sewing boxes. In the little front yards, pincushions shaped like flowers and mushrooms were growing; out of their tops colorful pinheads stuck up like little blossoms. Astonished, Emma noticed that the pins had faces. One of them winked at her; another yawned. Next to them were soft scraps of wool arranged like little sitting areas, and spools of thread were standing up straight like trees, letting their colorful threads flutter cheerfully in the wind. When a thread got loose and threatened to blow away, one of the spools would snatch at it lickety-split and tack it back down. Then the spool would doze off again. The gardens were really pretty. But where were the residents? Emma stood still and looked around her. Behind a house she saw something sparkle briefly; then it disappeared. Somebody was there.

"Hello?" called Emma. No one answered. She went farther, came to a screeching halt, and turned around with a jerk. That was an old gangster trick that she had seen once on television.

There! A little bit behind her stood a small silver thing wearing a gigantic red hat.

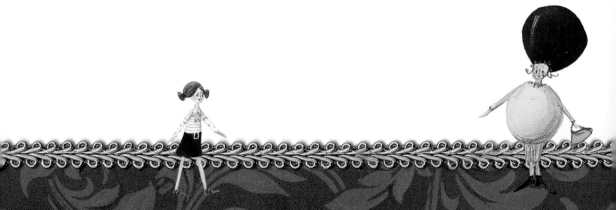

"Wait, please!" pleaded Emma. "I won't hurt you!" The thing stood still. Emma debated how she should address it.

"What a pretty button you are," she said cautiously. "And how stylish your hat is!"

"Isn't it!" said the thing, relieved. "I'm an original, the only one of my kind in the whole land!" It lowered its voice a little. "I believe I'm valuable, but I can't prove it. By the way, my name is Louise." Taking tiny little steps, Louise came closer.

"My name is Emma."

Louise extended her cold little hand toward Emma. Emma felt as though she were taking hold of a silver spoon.

"If I only knew how much I was worth," Louise continued. She sighed. Then she eyed Emma with interest. "You're not particularly valuable, are you?" she asked with sympathy.

"I don't know," said Emma, taken aback. Her mother always called her "my precious darling," but did that mean she was valuable?

"You don't look like a button either," Louise went on. "Or, are you something ultramodern? Where do you get fastened?"

"I don't get fastened." Emma almost laughed, but she managed to hold it back.

"You don't get fastened?" Louise's silvery eyes widened in amazement. "How can that be? I've never seen anything like you before. Are you sure you're not a button?"

Emma took a deep breath.

"I am not a button," she said quickly. "I'm a child."

"Not a button?" Louise's silvery mouth hung open. She swallowed. "And children don't have any hooks or loops or any holes in their stomachs? How odd!" She shook her head in bewilderment so that her heavy hat almost fell off.

"It's not good, not being a button," murmured Louise.

"Not good?" Emma felt a pang of anxiety. From a distance they heard a loud ruckus. Somebody was blowing a shrill whistle; a voice shouted, "She has to be here; I just saw her!"

Isolde! With icy fear Emma remembered that Isolde had intended to report her.

"Please, could you help me?" Emma reached for Louise's cool little hand. "I absolutely have to go back to where I came from. But I don't know how. And besides," she gulped in panic, "besides that, somebody's following me. Do you know where I could hide quickly?"

Louise nibbled on her silvery lower lip. Her little eyes darted back and forth uneasily.

"You're not a button; that's not good," she repeated softly, as if to herself. "You're a child without holes in your stomach. Whether that's good or not, I can't say. It's such a difficult question. You also seem to be made of a very strange material. Maybe you are valuable. Who knows?"

The ruckus kept coming closer. Apparently it involved a whole lot of buttons, because the pitter-patter of countless little feet could be heard.

At that moment, Emma had an idea. "If you help me, I'll find out how much you're worth!" she said, looking around anxiously.

"Oh, really?" Louise's mood improved suddenly. "You would do that?"

"Yes, of course!" Emma fidgeted with impatience. "But, we'd bet- ter get out of here, please."

"That goes without saying!"

Louise began to run so suddenly that Emma had trouble keeping up with her speedy legs. Moreover, Louise seemed to roll more than run.

They scurried along the blue path where they happened to meet a pair of tiny snap fasteners that were clearing fluff off the route.

"Out of the way!" shouted Louise. With a horrible clacking sound, the snap fasteners fell to the side. Emma tripped over one of them. Angrily, it shook its little fist.

Louise had already turned down an alley. There the road was made out of yellow velvet, and Emma would have liked to feel it, but there was no time. They ran and ran, and just as Emma thought she couldn't possibly take another step, Louise came to a sudden stop at a little house with a wooden bench in front.

A big, round, intricately carved button from a traditional German costume was sitting on it, eating a sausage sandwich. He looked at her in amazement.

"Gustav," called Louise. "This is Emma. If you help her hide, she'll find out if I'm valuable."

"Good day, ladies!" Gustav said, surprised. A few breadcrumbs were hanging on his mustache. He was a stag horn button, and whereas Louise's stomach was smooth, he was covered with white flowers.

"Edelweiss," he noted proudly, pointing to the flowers.

"Pretty," sputtered Emma. The ruckus made by the buttons was audible again. The carved button put his lunch aside and stood up.

"Then you'd better come in," he said, and opened the door. His hands were made out of smooth, white antler.

Emma darted inside Gustav's house.

And not one second too soon, because at that moment a throng of all kinds of buttons appeared—led by two uniform buttons and big golden Isolde. Emma looked cautiously out the window. The pack stopped short and seemed to deliberate. Then they ran on. Louise pressed her little silvery nose on the window next to Emma.

"Now, will you tell me how much I'm worth?" she whispered.

GUSTAV'S STORY

"Why is it so important to you to know how much you're worth?" Gustav asked, shaking his head at Louise. He pointed at a sofa, and Emma sat down. Amazed, Emma noticed that the sofa was sewn together from the oddest assortment of fabric scraps.

"It's important," Louise answered, stomping her foot. "Because that would show what my purpose is. If I belong on an exquisite princess's dress, perhaps, or . . . " She stopped.

"Or not," Gustav finished her sentence. Then he held up a finger. "The life's work of a button is to close something. Everything else is just frills. Right?" He turned abruptly to Emma.

"Frills," Emma repeated obediently. Then something occurred to her. "But you must know where you come from," she said, turning back to Louise. "I mean, you must have been on a dress or a jacket at one time?"

Louise hung her head.

"No, I never was," she whispered, and her silvery lips quivered a little. "I was always a spare button."

"Oh," said Emma, embarrassed.

Gustav cleared his throat.

"Not every button is as lucky as I am," he said. "I had the chance to live on one of the most splendid pieces of clothing in the world, to see the world, to fall in love . . . " He looked off wistfully into the distance.

Emma felt a little uneasy. She had the feeling that at any moment both buttons could burst into tears. As for herself, she wanted nothing more than to get big again.

"What kind of clothing was it?" she asked politely.

Gustav sniffled a little and stroked his flower carvings with pride.

"Lederhosen," he said. You could see that the question had pleased him.

"I was on a pair of lederhosen made out of the finest goat leather, with suspenders and embroidery." He smiled at the memory. "As everyone knows, landing on lederhosen is the best of luck for a button. They're almost indestructible. I had my spot on the left suspender for thirty-four years. It was a wonderful time."

"How lovely," said Emma. Neither she nor her mother had ever owned a pair of lederhosen. In the meantime, Louise had climbed up on the couch next to Emma and nestled up coolly against her.

"We lived on a farm in the mountains," continued Gustav. "It smelled like meadow, woods, and sometimes like cows too.

The man who wore us liked to sing while he worked. We buttons sang along. That's when I first noticed her. The exquisite carved button on the right suspender. She had the loveliest voice in the world. One night I got up all my courage and spoke to her. Her name was

Constance. We became a couple. For years we told each other the most beautiful stories, enjoyed life until . . . until . . . "

Gustav's voice failed.

"Until?" asked Emma and Louise in unison.

Gustav took a deep breath. "Our owner got older and older and didn't go out as much. Most of the time we just hung in the closet, but it wasn't so bad. It was comfortable and warm. However, one day he took the lederhosen out again and put them on. This time we took the train into a big city. It was unbelievably exciting, but awfully crowded too. There was always somebody bumping into our poor owner, and all of a sudden I noticed something horrible."

Emma held her breath.

"I felt that I couldn't hold on tight anymore. With every step I got looser. And then, in the middle of the market square, I got light-headed and dizzy, and I fell off. Constance was still shouting my name; then she was gone. The owner of the lederhosen simply went on and didn't even notice that I had fallen off. He was just too old." Big tears were running down Gustav's face now.

"That's just awful," said Emma, clearly distressed. She hadn't known until now how tragic it was to lose a button!

"The rest was quick. I lay for a while in the dirt in the street, until a big man picked me up, took me with him, and brought me here."

"Uncle Hubert!" Emma shouted at once.

"Since then I've lived here, and although it's not a bad existence, I still yearn for an active life. Smelling the woods and meadows again! Seeing Constance once again!"

"I envy you anyway, Gustav. You've experienced so much. I haven't experienced anything; I'm just waiting." Louise sighed.

"I'm waiting too," Emma said. "For my mother."

"Oh?" asked Gustav. "Is that your owner?"

"No, she's my mother. I'm a child. My mother is in Africa."

Louise looked at her blankly. "Are there buttons in Africa?" she asked.

Emma didn't know if there were buttons in Africa. "There are lions there," she answered, unsure.

Gustav observed her thoughtfully.

"So, you're not a button?" he asked at last.

Emma shook her head.

"Can't you help me get big again?" she asked. "Or show me the way back to the big room? Maybe I can help you find Constance again?"

Gustav seemed to think it over. Lost in thought, he scratched his head.

"Perhaps," he began, "there is somebody who can help us."

"Oh, really?" Emma felt extremely relieved.

"I don't know if he can make you big again, but he has a bunch

of strange guests. Also lots of," Gustav lowered his voice, "non-buttons." He opened the door a crack. "The coast is clear," he said. "Come on, we'll give it a try. I've already sat around here far too long doing nothing. That won't bring Constance back."

"Thank you so much, dear Gustav!" Emma wanted to give him a hug. "And I promise you, when I get big again, I'll find a new pair of lederhosen for you, word of honor!"

Gustav smiled a little sadly. "That's nice of you. But without my Constance, it wouldn't be the same."

He pushed Emma out the door.

"I'm coming too!" said Louise firmly. "You still haven't told me if I'm valuable!"

WITH THE HIPPIES

Gustav, Louise, and Emma ran for a while along a road; this time, the road was green as grass and silky, and rustled with every step. Dusk was falling already, and all around them streetlights were turning on. Emma noticed that the lights were upside-down thimbles.

"Where are we going?" she whispered. Gustav didn't answer. He ran ahead with sure steps, his white antler feet in thick, practical hiking shoes. He was almost racing. Louise was rolling effortlessly behind; it was just Emma who could barely keep up.

"Are we almost there?" Emma gasped, as they finally came to a stop. Gustav nodded.

"Just down Tape Measure Road," he said quietly. Sure enough, instead of a fence on their right, there was an un-rolled tape measure, reaching as far as the eye could see.

And then, just as Emma was thinking that she would have to spend the rest of her life with these two, tramping along this road, Gustav stopped. They had reached their goal, a gray box building.

It wasn't a particularly beautiful house. Actually, Emma noticed now, it wasn't even a regular house, just an old shoebox where you throw all your junk that doesn't belong anywhere else. Gustav gave the door three quick raps. It wobbled alarmingly. Emma would

have preferred to back away. If the house collapsed, golden Isolde would turn up here in no time with her police guards. Then the door opened, and an oblong wooden button stood before them. He was wearing a poncho and had a headband around his head.

"Peace, man!" he said to them.

"Evening, sir," replied Gustav with dignity. "We need to ask for your help. I'm looking for my fiancée, Constance. Louise, here, would like to find out if she's valuable. And Emma is an extremely special case. Not a button. Definitely not a button. Says she's a child. Now that, of course, can't be. Children are normally bigger. However, there is a certain similarity to a child."

The wooden button looked Emma over kindly. "Welcome to our commune, strange thing. I'm Woody!" he greeted her. A funny smell, a little bit like the smell from incense burners, wafted out of the house. Somebody was playing guitar and singing.

"Commune?" Emma had never heard the word before.

"Here at our place everybody's equal," he explained. "Buttons, nonbuttons, it's all the same to us. We're hippies. I was personally there at Woodstock; that explains my name. Peace. Flower Power and so on."

"What?" Emma asked, baffled.

"Woodstock," said Woody. "The music festival! Duh, you've never heard of it?"

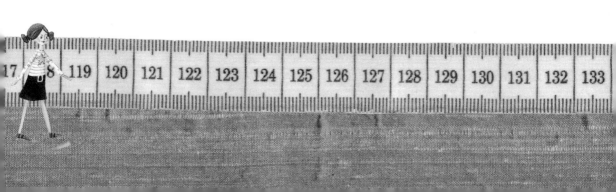

Emma shook her head. Was that something you were supposed to know?

"What's your name again, thingy?" asked Woody. He sounded a little offended.

"Emma," said Emma.

Woody clapped his hands enthusiastically. "That was the name of the owner of the cardigan I used to live on! She played a terrific harmonica. Come in!" With that, he pushed her into the house. Emma found herself in a huge room, which was decorated from top to bottom with colorful fabric ribbons. All over the place the strangest figures were sitting on soft pillows; some were even lying on the floor. Candles were burning, and from the ceiling somebody had hung silvery threads, which were turning to and fro.

"How pretty!" said Emma, impressed.

"Are those valuable?" asked Louise breathlessly, pointing to the silver threads.

"As if that were important!" said somebody next to them. Emma looked up in surprise. What was standing in front of her was definitely not a button. It was a wiry little man.

"What are you?" Emma asked curiously. The little man gasped for breath. The entire room became silent. Emma noticed that every eye was on her.

"What am I?" The little man stretched and became almost twice as tall. His voice almost cracked. "Dear Emma-thing, if I knew that, I would not be here, would I? At any rate, I'm not a button!" He burst out in a short, bitter laugh.

Woody waved his hands soothingly. "Peace, love, harmony, friends!" he exclaimed. "Maybe the Emma-thing can help us after all."

Emma examined the little man. Something about him looked familiar. Of course! "I think," she said in a firm voice, "you're a paper clip."

Somebody dropped a glass, which broke with a shatter.

"A what?" whispered the little man.

"A paper clip. You know, you use it to hold papers together. In offices. Or when you're doing crafts." Emma thought it would have been easier to grab him and use him to hold something or other together in order to explain it to him better. But to her dismay, she saw that tears were running down the little man's thin, wiry face.

"I'm sorry," Emma stammered, shocked. "I didn't mean to offend you, I . . . "

"Dear Emma-thingy," sniffed the paper clip. "You haven't offended me. You've made me the happiest creature in the world. I'm a paper clip! I have a purpose! I hold papers together! How lovely!"

Cheers broke out all around them.

Everyone crowded around Emma.

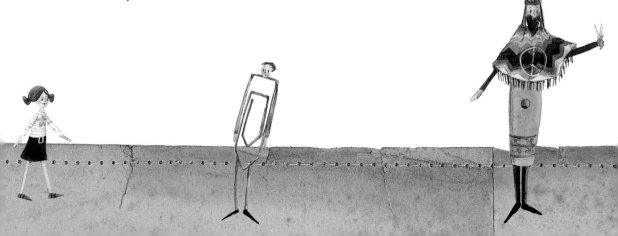

"What am I?" they yelled. "Please, help me too! I've been trying for so long to find out what I really am!"

Emma held her hands up in defense.

Woody pushed through the crowd. "Quiet! You'll all get your turn," he bellowed to all those standing around. Then he turned back to Emma. "You'll have to excuse them. It's so seldom that somebody comes by who can give us information. Most of those who are

staying here have no idea what they are. Or they've forgotten after all this time. They just know that they're not buttons. And that's why they have to serve buttons. Polish shoes for big gold buttons or stand around all day and be garden ornaments." He sighed. The others nodded sadly.

"One time, there was somebody here who looked a lot like you," the paper clip mused. "Now that I know what I am, it just occurred to me."

"Another child?" asked Emma, astonished. Maybe there was another girl or boy here who could help her.

"No, that thing didn't say it was a child." The paper clip seemed to be thinking it over. "It had the same shape as you, I'm sure of that. But it had red wool on its head."

"Oh," said Emma, disappointed. Red wool on its head did not suggest a child.

"And it howled and yammered the whole time," the paper clip

continued. "It really got on everybody's nerves. It complained constantly that it would miss dinner."

"What happened to it?" asked Emma.

The paper clip shrugged his slightly bent shoulders. "No idea. I only remember that everyone was happy when the thing suddenly disappeared."

"It doesn't matter now," another little man butted in. "Tell us what we are instead!"

"Well, now, I can take a look at all of you," Emma said kindly. She studied the little man.

"You're obviously a stone! And you back there, you're a sea shell." Impressed murmuring resounded. "And you up front in the second row, you're a coin! A coin; people can go shopping with you." The coin sank to its knees and threw its hands up in silent rejoicing.

"What?" Emma heard a little voice in her ear. "What did you say? Is he valuable?" Louise was standing next to her, uneasy, wringing her silvery hands.

"Certainly not as valuable as you," Emma said quickly. Then she continued. "You're a cap for a felt-tip marker, you're a snail shell, and you're an eraser."

"Where I come from, there are big rooms . . . lands," she corrected herself, "where snail shells live. Or stones. If you help me to get back there, I can bring you to your relatives."

"Promise?" asked the little stone.

Emma nodded. "Can you help me?"

For a long while, an embarrassed silence reigned. Then Woody shook his head in resignation. "I don't think so," he said. "We have no idea where these room-lands are, or how you get to them. But you can stay with us. Forever!" His eyes lit up, and his headband slipped in the excitement.

Emma let out a soft sigh. Certainly the hippies were very nice, but she really wanted to become a child again and not just be referred to as "Emma-thingy." Besides that, she had promised Gustav and Louise her help. And there was still sneaky Isolde to watch out for.

All of a sudden, a clear voice chimed, "I know who can help you."

All heads whipped around. Emma looked in surprise at a gorgeous white button made of lace, tulle, and satin.

"Who can help us?"

"There is only one who can help us, who knows everything. Big V."

"Oh no! For heaven's sake! Not Big V!" echoed throughout the room.

The white button's smile was mocking. "Maybe you're scared?" she asked.

"Of course not, Miranda," said Woody. "But Big V, Big V is . . . " He faltered.

"Is what?" asked Emma.

"Our enemy!" whispered Woody. "The enemy of all buttons."

THE CASTAWAY BRIDE

Everyone in the room fell silent in fear. Emma would have loved to find out more about this mysterious V, but it didn't seem to be a good idea to keep probing. Even the dark blue felt-tip marker cap had turned pale.

"You must be tired," said the pretty white button, whom Woody had addressed as Miranda. "And of course you're hungry too." She clapped her delicate hands, sending a wisp of powder from her gloves into the air. Two flat things carried a tray of baked goods into the room. Emma bent over in order to get a better look at them.

"You're tickets," she said, taken aback. "And not even stamped yet. Somebody could use you to ride the streetcar!"

The tickets began to tremble so much in surprise that they dropped the tray. "Unstamped," they said over and over again, stunned. "Not stamped yet. What luck!" Then they dragged themselves back into the corner and told each other where they would want to go if somebody stamped them.

Miranda carefully picked up a roll from the floor and handed it to Emma. "Didn't get dirty."

"Thanks, you're very kind." Emma bit off a big piece. Miranda smiled and seemed friendly, so Emma attempted to find out more.

"So, who is this Big V?" she asked in a quiet voice. The last thing

she wanted was for everybody in the room to stop breathing or for somebody to break the dishes.

Miranda glanced quickly from left to right. Then she bent toward Emma. "He's big. Bigger than all of us. Box-shaped, with horrible teeth. He never lets go of anybody he gets a hold of. A while ago, a poor little fuzz got too close to him, and he snapped shut. We never saw the fuzz again."

Emma shuddered. Not only was the vicious Isolde here, not only was it for unknown reasons bad not to be a button, but there was also a dreadful monster you had to beware of.

"That certainly is horrible," she blurted.

Miranda batted her eyes. "Now, the secret is not to come too close to him. Then nothing happens to you. The fuzz was very reckless and curious. What's more, V is insanely clever. He knows more than all of us put together. And he can do the work of five buttons at the same time."

"Work?" Emma couldn't really grasp what the buttons worked at all day.

Miranda skittered back and forth impatiently. "Closing things, of course. Big V has five times more power to close things than we have. That's why everyone's afraid of him. If he does such a wonderful job of closing things, and on top of that gobbles up all his enemies, eventually there will be no more buttons."

Emma frowned. Big V seemed to be a very peculiar thing. She could not for the life of her imagine what it was all about. And although Miranda's description sounded rather scary, she still had an overwhelming desire to meet him and ask how she could get back home again.

She was thinking over exactly how best to do that when somebody breathed warm air into her ear. It was Louise, who had sat down noiselessly behind her and was staring at Miranda as though hypnotized. Behind Louise's cool metal forehead, there was a lot going on. Emma could just imagine what was on her mind. Then Louise fired off her question to Miranda: "You're so sparkly. Could it be that you're valuable?"

For a moment, Miranda looked terribly sad. "No," she said. "No, I'm not. I was once very valuable to somebody. But that time is past."

"How do you figure that?" asked Louise, quite anxious. "Can you be valuable at one time and then not be valuable anymore? That would be awful! Where does the value go?"

Miranda smiled glumly. "I haven't figured that out. I'm not made of valuable material, if that's what you think. Just a little bit of satin with pearly embroidery. But once I was the most beautiful thing in the world to my owner."

"Were you on a pair of lederhosen too?" asked Louise.

"Of course not," retorted Miranda. "Do I look like I belonged to a farmer in the mountains?" She sniffed. "I was a decorative button on a wedding gown."

"Oh," said Emma and Louise at the same time. "How romantic."

"Yes, it was. We satin buttons formed a decorative strip on the front of the dress. What a to-do that was! What giggling and fidgeting! The seamstress warned us over and over again throughout the day to hold still while she was sewing the dress. It was hanging on a wooden stand, but often the future bride came by to try it on. Then she would tell us about her sweetheart. She was crazy about him. His name was Hannes." Miranda smiled, misty-eyed. "Once, he had a bouquet of red roses sent to her. They smelled wonderful. And then one day the dress was ready. It looked like a dream, especially because of us decorative buttons, obviously. We could all admire ourselves in the full-length mirror. Our owner came early in the morning, all rosy-cheeked, and put the dress on." Miranda stopped talking.

"And then?" asked Emma. "How was the wedding? Was there yummy cake?" She had been a flower girl herself once for one of her mother's friends and remembered only too well a three-foot-high marzipan cake.

A white glitter-tear rolled down Miranda's cheek. "There was no wedding," she whispered.

"For real?" asked Louise. "It wasn't a wedding gown at all? Was it a nightgown? Nightgowns can be closed with buttons."

"Obviously it was a wedding gown! But there was no wedding because there was no bridegroom! Handsome Hannes walked out on her and ran off with a woman from the bowling club. A woman so incredibly fat that there aren't even any wedding gowns in her size!" Miranda stamped her foot in fury and wailed at the top of her lungs. Emma and Louise didn't know what to say.

"Didn't she . . . didn't the bride just keep the dress? For the next . . . " Emma cleared her throat, embarrassed.

"That's bad luck! Don't you know that?" Miranda snapped at her. "No. She didn't want to see the dress again. So it got cut up, and we buttons ended up in the drawer."

For a while they sat in silence; only the noise made by the others filled the room.

Louise mulled it over. "I bet," she remarked shrewdly, "the dress wasn't valuable enough for the bridegroom!"

At that moment somebody outside pounded loudly on the cardboard door.

"Open up!" thundered a rough voice. "Open up immediately! Police!"

THE MYSTYERIOUS V

Two golden uniform buttons barged into the room. One was small and round; the other long and thin. The thinner one looked a little shabby. In his excitement, he waved a roll of paper.

"Are there any non-buttonth here?" he bellowed.

"What do you mean?" asked Gustav.

"Ith there anybody here who ithn't a button?" screeched the uniform button. Emma couldn't help chuckling, even though she was scared.

"That one!" roared the police officer. "The one over there! She ithn't a button! Come with uth!"

"Wh . . . what?" stammered Emma, frightened. Why hadn't she just hidden quickly like the others—the paper clip, the tickets, the stones, even the coin had all disappeared.

The big round uniform button elbowed his way pompously to the front, pushing his colleague to the side. He reached into his pocket and pulled out a pair of glasses, which he tried to put on his nose, but they kept slipping down his smooth face. "Who are you?" he growled at Emma. "And what are you?"

Emma made a polite curtsey.

"My name is Emma." She didn't get any further.

Both uniform buttons stared at her. Then they put their heads together, making a clanking sound.

"She ithn't a button," Emma heard the long one whisper.

"But I'm the boss," retorted the big round one. "I ask the questions here."

"Why ith that?"

"Because I'm more golden and shiny than you, that's why."

"But you got to arretht the latht prisonerth. Now I want to!"

The round button swung his sword around unsteadily. Then he said to his colleague, "Good, then say 'sword.'"

"Thword."

"See, you can't do it. And as long as you can't say 'sword,' you're not allowed to arrest anyone!"

Emma thought these police officers had a strange way of deciding things, but she stayed quiet as a mouse. Louise shoved her little hand into Emma's, and Gustav stood in front of her protectively.

The paper clip's long head poked out from behind a cabinet. Emma hoped the police wouldn't see him. But it was too late.

"There!" yelled the thin one, all excited. "There'th one! Behind the cabinet!" And the other buttons and nonbuttons were so curious that they all came out of their hiding places.

"You're all arrested!" screamed the big round one. "We're looking for a nonbutton who claims to be a child. And since we don't know what a child is, it could be any of you, right?"

Emma held her breath in fear. But the others stayed quiet, either

because they didn't want to betray Emma, or because they were so afraid that they had already forgotten what a child was.

"In any cathe," piped up the thin police officer with a shrill voice, "you're all coming with uth right now. That'th an order!"

"You don't get to give orders," said the big round button with quiet authority.

"I . . . " The thin police officer blinked in confusion and held his tongue.

"We won't leave you alone," whispered Louise in Emma's ear. "We'll come along! And help you!"

"Thank you," Emma whispered back. But she still felt a little scared, even though both police officers were being really ridiculous.

"Everybody line up," the round one ordered. They all followed orders and lined up. "You, you, you, and you—come along!" he said, prodding each nonbutton in the stomach.

"Peace, friends," Woody called, distraught. "How about a cup of tea? Or some tambourine music? Or an itty-bit of peace pipe?"

"Get out of my way thith minute!" ordered the thin one.

"No, the blockhead should get out of my way. Don't forget that you don't have anything to say about that," the big round one butted in.

The thin one twisted his mouth in a huff.

Shaking her head, Emma followed the strange long line made up

of little stones, tickets, snail shells, and paper clips out into the dark night. The patter of countless tinny feet clattered on the road they were taking, because, as Emma discovered, it was crocheted from little metal hooks and eyes.

"Where are they taking us?" somebody yammered.

"Gustav and I are right behind you," said Louise softly to Emma.

Nevertheless, the big round police officer had heard her. He reeled around and eyed her. "You're a button," he stated. "And that one, too!" He pointed an accusing finger at Gustav. "We have orders to bring only nonbuttons!" His golden suit sparkled in the moonlight, and Emma could clearly make out an anchor embossed on his stomach. An anchor? Emma had never seen a police officer with anchor buttons. Weren't anchors actually on uniforms of. . . .

"Hey! You two foolish sailors," rang out a loud, assertive voice. The little procession jerked to a stop. A big dark shadow was vaguely noticeable in front of them. It moved.

"Mommy," peeped one of the tickets.

"What'th going on?" the thin police officer frantically yelled.

"Let the prisoners go free! Otherwise you'll have some real trouble on your hands!"

"Oh, yeah?"

The big round police officer wasn't so easily intimidated. "And with whom, please? And what do you mean by sailors? We are police officers!"

"You're sailor buttons. Haven't you ever asked yourselves why you have an anchor on your stomachs, hmm?"

"Tho that we don't drift away in the water?" the thin one considered.

"Shut your trap!" hissed the round one. In a loud voice he said, "At any rate, we're not saying anything in front of some tramp. You're not even showing yourself to us!"

"Oh, you'd like to see me?" sneered the voice. "That can be arranged!"

A murmur went through the crowd, when, as though out of nothing, a big black square appeared before them. It had tiny arms, but oodles of spiny bristles on its front.

"It'th Big V! Big V," shrieked the thin police officer, horrified. He took a giant leap backward and ran away as quickly as his rickety legs could carry him.

Panic broke out. Everyone fell topsy-turvy all over each other; they screeched and floundered around, while, in the background, the round police officer blew nervously on his whistle.

Emma, however, had looked at the mysterious V intently and began to laugh out loud. She laughed so hard that she fell onto the crocheted road and pinned down one of the tickets.

"Help!" he cried, causing most of the nonbuttons to run away in fear, the big round police officer ahead of all of them.

"Everyone," Emma called with amusement. "Come back!" She held on tightly to Louise and Gustav, who also wanted to make themselves scarce. "Louise, Gustav, listen to me! Big V isn't dangerous." Emma took a deep breath so that she didn't get the hiccups from laughing. "He's only a Velcro fastener!"

"You recognized me?" The enormous Velcro fastener smiled. "How happy that makes me!"

"Yes, of course," said Emma. "I like Velcro. It's so nice and fast. *Scritch, scritch,* and the shoe is off. Or the jacket. Much easier than buttons. Because . . . " She stopped and bit her lip, because Gustav's face had gotten whiter than before, and Louise was shaking so much that her hat was wobbling alarmingly.

"She likes Velcro," said Big V dreamily, as if to himself. "Today is my lucky day. And here I just wanted to frighten the silly sailor buttons." He gave a short laugh. "They don't know what they are, but they want to play policeman. And then I meet this little thing who loves Velcro!" He yanked out a handkerchief as big as a bed sheet and gently dabbed his eyes.

There was no doubt—he was crying! A fat tear rolled down his bristly cheek. Then he reached out to Emma with a hand attached to a skinny little arm.

"Don't touch him!" whispered Louise. "He wants to gobble you up!"

"Nonsense," said Emma. "You might get caught on him for a moment, that's all. Like on the little hooks of a burr. That's why he can also be called a hook-and-loop fastener."

49

"Are you sure?" asked Gustav, who was so nervous that he kept rubbing his edelweiss design.

Instead of answering, Emma grabbed the Velcro's hand and gave it a hearty shake. Then she touched his rough surface, which felt like a hairbrush. Louise squeaked softly in fright.

"What's your name, you unspeakably smart thing?" asked the Velcro.

"Emma. And you? Big V isn't really your name, is it?"

"No." He turned a little red.

Emma waited. "Well?" she asked then.

"My name is Victor."

"That's a very nice name," said Emma. "Why didn't you ever tell that to the buttons? And why are they all afraid of you?"

"Well, I tried to be their friend at first!" Victor waved his hand as he explained. "I told them how terrific I am at closing things. I thought they'd be happy that we had something in common! But that only frightened them. And then one day, this stupid fuzz came along and wanted to fight with me. I couldn't let myself get beaten by a fuzz!"

He stopped talking, embarrassed.

"What did you do with him?" asked Gustav, his voice hoarse.

"Absolutely nothing! The silly thing got caught in my bristles and just didn't come back out. I couldn't help him; you can see for yourself how useless my hands are!"

Victor stretched out his tiny little hands in front, and, sure enough, they didn't reach his stomach. "The fuzz grumbled and wailed for days and got himself even more tangled up. And then one day he fell off. He yelled at me furiously and ran away. Nobody has seen him since, and now all the buttons think I'm a monster." Victor folded up in the middle and sat down on the side of the road with a loud ripping sound. Emma, Louise, and Gustav cautiously sat down next to him. It was indeed a sad fate. The moon shone on the sparkling road, and in the distance a sewing machine rolled along a track.

Emma cleared her throat. "Are there more . . . of your kind?" she asked.

Victor shook his rectangular head in distress. "No. There were four of us once. We lived on a student's backpack. A fine bag it was. *Scritch, scratch,* it opened—*scritch, scratch,* it closed. He never lost a thing. That was our contribution."

"That goes for buttons too," observed Gustav.

"Anyway, we went to the most excellent lectures with him. We learned everything there was to learn about books. Ask me something—anything!"

"Do your bristles hurt?" asked Louise.

Victor looked a little disappointed. "I meant, ask me something about books!"

"Oh." Emma thought it over. "What is your favorite book?

"Ah! Good question. There was a book about a man, who lived all alone on an island. His name was Robinson, and he was very lonely. I liked that." He lowered his voice. "I think about that a lot."

"Where . . . where is the bag now?" asked Emma, although she was a little afraid of the answer. It couldn't be good; otherwise Victor wouldn't be so sad.

"In the used clothes bin," said Victor, in a matter-of-fact tone. "One day our student was finished with his studies and bought himself a glossy black briefcase. The old bag had gotten too shabby for him; he threw it away. Fortunately, his granny had at least taken us Velcro fasteners off. She thought they were something the lad could still use. But he didn't want any Velcro on his new briefcase. And so we four got separated. And that was just when we had formed a literary quartet."

"A literary quartet?" That meant nothing to Emma.

"Well, since we couldn't go to lectures anymore, we started composing poems ourselves. It was generally said that my poems were the best." Victor coyly cleared his throat. "Would you like to hear one?"

"Yes," said Emma.

"Please do," Gustav requested.

"If it has to be," said Louise.

Victor ignored her. He took a deep breath. "The Bag," he began solemnly:

A water bottle, old and smashed
lies in the bottom of the bag.
In the lining, way in back,
a pencil's stuck inside a snag.
Some books and gloves,
mints—slightly sticky
plus dried-up gum
that's really icky.
Every day new stuff goes in,
like tickets, candy, safety pin.
But who's important, without a doubt,
for keeping things from falling out?

The Velcro's voice got louder and louder with the last words. Emma, Louise, and Gustav stared at him with their mouths open.

"Who?" Gustav whispered with hushed expectation.

Victor threw his little arm up dramatically and shouted:

Who is this hero of the day?
The Velcro holds it closed! Hurray!

For a moment there was a dead silence. Victor took a little bow.

"Brilliant," Emma burst out finally.

"Each as he is able," murmured Louise.

"May I ask what material the bag was made of?" Gustav asked. "Was it perhaps goat leather? Because . . . " Suddenly he paused. "Do you hear that?" he whispered. A slight distance away, the big round police officer's whistle could be heard.

"They're thtill here!" That was clearly the thin police officer again!

"Come," said Victor, without further ado. "Climb into my bristles. When I close up, nobody will see you."

"But will we come back out again?" Louise's voice was hoarse with fear. "Because I wouldn't like getting stuck for days, like the fuzz! I still have to figure out my value and place in life."

"I must look for my beloved Constance," Gustav reminded them.

"And I want to get back home," said Emma. She still hadn't gotten around to asking Victor if he had any idea how she could get back to the button room.

At that moment, the bright light of a flashlight shone in the bushes. The police officers were there already, and it sounded as if they had brought along backup.

"Let's go!" ordered Emma. She snatched Louise's hand, locked arms with Gustav, and got set to take a big jump.

"Alley-oop!" Victor yelled. Emma could feel her legs landing on a sticky, bristly base. And just as the flashlight's beam landed on Victor, he scrunched himself together.

"Well, you silly sailors!" he yelled. "Haven't you had enough yet?" Then he got moving and ran off with huge steps, so that it was impossible for the police officers to follow him. It was comfortable sitting deep inside the Velcro. Like in a train chugging along—and Emma fell into a deep sleep.

GOOD ADVICE

Emma didn't wake up until the sun was shining through Victor's bristles. She stretched, and her hand hit Gustav, who was still sleeping.

"Constance, my dearest," he murmured in his dream. Louise's eyes were still closed too; her hands were on her hat. Emma gingerly stroked the ruby red stone. It sparkled mysteriously in the early morning light, and all of a sudden Emma could understand Louise's yearning to find out if she was valuable. At any rate, this hat was something quite special.

"Have a good night's sleep?" Victor's voice droned from above. With a loud scritch he opened his fastener. Quite suddenly it got so bright that Emma had to squint. Gustav muttered something or other, annoyed.

"Where are we?" Emma asked Victor.

"In a meadow," he replied. "Isn't it a gorgeous day?"

Emma looked around. The meadow was unbelievably beautiful—nothing but soft woolen strands in all different shades of green. Then she noticed that Victor was holding a pen and a piece of paper in his hand. "What are you doing?"

"I'm writing a poem. A sunny morning like this one must be immortalized on paper. I have the first line already." He rustled the paper a little. "Bright shines the sun on the land of buttons—"

"While you're on the subject," Emma interrupted him, "I absolutely have to get back home. You see, I don't come from Buttonland."

"Of course not. A blind man could see that," Victor said. Then he took another breath. "Bright shines the sun on the land of buttons . . . Nothing comes to mind here that rhymes with buttons."

"Gluttons," said Emma mechanically. "But Victor, do you know how I can get back to the land of people? I'm not a button, and I have to get back, so that I can see my mother when vacation is over." The thought of her mother almost brought Emma to tears. What if she had to spend the rest of her life among paper clips and tickets?

"Gluttons! You really are unbelievably smart. That's why I'm a little surprised that you haven't come up with the solution to your problem on your own."

"How?" asked Emma, bewildered.

"Now, the question is—how did you get here, hmm? You should be able to get back exactly the same way."

Emma thought it over. "Well," she hesitated. "I went into the button room in my aunt's house and saw the fat gold button, I mean, Lady Isolde. Then she ran around and talked to me. That is to say, she scolded me," Emma corrected herself. "And I wanted this talking button, so I lay down on my stomach and stuck out my arm and

touched Isolde, and then . . . then all of a sudden I was here."

"Well, you see!" Victor exclaimed cheerfully. "Then you must find Isolde and touch her again, and you'll end up back home!" He shook his square head in amusement and bent down, turning his attention to his poem once more.

Emma couldn't believe what she was hearing. Could it really be so simple? And didn't that mean that she had to find the dreadful Isolde—after trying to run away from her all this time? And how was she supposed to touch Isolde without getting sent right to jail?

"Where will I find Isolde then?" she asked, rather unhappy.

"At the castle," said Victor. "You can find everything at the castle."

"Even Constance?" asked Gustav, who was listening to their conversation.

"Certainly," said Victor, although he didn't know who or what Constance was.

"And at the castle they'll certainly know if Louise is valuable," said Emma.

"Really? Really? You mean we just need to go to the castle, and then finally I'll find out?" asked Louise from inside the Velcro bristles. Carefully she climbed out. "Let's get going!"

"Yes, let's get going," echoed Gustav. "How do we get to the castle?"

Victor paused. "That, my dear friends, unfortunately I cannot tell you. I only know that it's on an island in a lake."

"In a lake? There's a lake here?" asked Emma, amazed.

"Well, why not?" the others asked at the same time.

"Naturally, why not," Emma agreed. And why shouldn't there be a lake? There was a castle, after all!

"Bright shines the sun on the land of buttons; to the castle march the three nice gluttons." Victor waved his paper in delight. "That's good," he murmured to himself. "That is amazingly good." Then he looked up. "If it makes no difference to you, I'd rather be alone so I can finish this poem."

"Of course." Gustav went down first, hand over hand, along Victor's bristles. Emma and Louise went down after him. It was quite easy; they just had to watch out so they didn't get caught. That was something the poor little fuzz probably hadn't realized.

"Good-bye, Victor," said Emma once she was on the ground again. "You've helped us so much. I hope that I can help you too sometime."

Victor gnawed on his pen.

"I'd like to get my poets' quartet back. But that's probably impossible."

"Maybe I could look into it for you when I'm big again," Emma offered.

But Victor shook his square head. "They're long gone. That's the way of the world." He took a quick nibble on the pen. "Muttons," he said dreamily. "Muttons also rhymes with buttons."

Louise, Gustav, and Emma looked at each other and shrugged their shoulders. Then they set off to find the lake. But all around them there was nothing to see except soft cotton grass and knitted trees that were beginning to unravel.

"I'm hungry," said Louise after a little while.

Gustav stopped so suddenly that Emma collided with him. Without a word, he pointed straight ahead. There were the crocheted streets again. And—Emma could hardly believe it—a huge trailer with a light blue awning over the window, and the most scrumptious aromas pouring out.

"Yarny's Snack Bar" Emma read. "Fresh, delicious, good." She cheered with delight.

"It's about time," remarked Louise.

MIMI AND KITTY

In the snack bar sat a gray skein of yarn. She looked a bit worn-out already; a strand was hanging loosely down her side. Deeply absorbed, she was studying the magazine *Stitch 'n' Knit*, moving her lips silently.

"Still closed," she grumbled without looking up as the three came closer, and Gustav knocked on the trailer.

"I'm dying of hunger," Louise whispered. "What's good here?"

"No idea," said Emma. "But it smells yummy."

"Like schnitzel," said Gustav. "In that case, I'll have schnitzel as soon as it's open."

"Did you hear that, Kitty?" asked someone behind them. Emma whirled around. Two big button ladies with gold decorations and long sparkling legs were standing there. One was holding a little purple purse in her hand; the other one was wearing big sunglasses. The one with the sunglasses let out a horrified little cry. "Do you actually know how fat you get from eating schnitzel?" She turned to Gustav.

"Fat?" Gustav frowned, dumbfounded.

"Fat," repeated the button with the sunglasses, apparently Kitty. "Horribly fat. Porky. Flabby, chubby-cheeked."

"But it's delicious," replied Gustav, astonished.

Kitty raised a delicate finger, on which at least three rings were sparkling. "Delicious it is. But just for a short time. And after that, then what?"

Both buttons shook their heads, making their earrings jingle. "A moment on the lips, a lifetime on the hips," they chorused. They gave each other a high five. There was a loud jingling.

"Who are you?" asked Emma.

"You can't tell?" Kitty seemed to be shocked. "You don't recognize us?"

"No," answered Emma. Maybe they were ladies too?

The button lady with the handbag stretched a little. On her flat purple stomach were two intertwined Cs.

"So?" she asked impatiently. "Has it dawned on you yet?"

"Your name is Cecile?" asked Louise. "And your last name is Cesar?"

The button rolled her eyes.

"You two are Cornelia and Claudia?" asked Emma.

"Chanel, you dummies!" Kitty barked at her. "We're Chanel buttons! Models! I'm Kitty; that's Mimi."

"Chanel? Is that valuable?" asked Louise.

"Of course it's valuable," Kitty retorted snippily.

Impressed, Louise fell silent.

"Chanel is the most elegant fashion house in Paris. We were on

unbelievably expensive jackets and skirts," continued Kitty. "We met the most wonderful designers and were on the greatest runways in the world—Paris, Rome, Milan, New York, at London Fashion Week . . . "

"But not anymore," Louise observed. "Did you fall off too, like Gustav?"

"Open now," said the skein of yarn suddenly from the snack bar. She hadn't moved from the spot the whole time.

"Two waters, please. And a lettuce leaf," Kitty demanded right away.

"We were here first," grumbled Gustav.

Mimi smiled indulgently. "Of course, you were here first. But certainly you don't have to get to a fashion show right away"—after a quick check of her polished fingernail—"the way you look." Kitty jabbed her in the ribs. There was a little clacking noise.

With a crabby face, the skein of yarn handed out two cups of water from the trailer.

"Goodness gracious," squeaked Mimi and glanced at her glistening wristwatch. "I think we'll have to pass on the lettuce. The show is about to start!"

"It's better this way," said Kitty. "We don't want to overeat. Otherwise we won't fit into our outfits anymore." They both let out a short, shrill laugh and got ready to go.

"Wait," called Emma. "Do you know how to get to the lake? We want to go to the castle."

"To the castle? Wearing that?"

Kitty wrinkled her sparkling little nose, horrified.

"Yes, how else?" asked Gustav. "These are practical hiking shoes. Much more practical than your high heels."

"But not chic," peeped Kitty.

"The hat on that one is okay," Mimi whispered to her friend, pointing to Louise. "They'll probably let her in. But the other two . . . " She rolled her eyes again.

"It's a long way to the lake," said Kitty. "And if I were you, I'd freshen up a bit." She pointed in the direction of the street and tugged on Mimi's arm.

"It'll take a while. Before that, you'll go through a funny town with nothing but people whose taste is as bad as yours," observed Mimi. They both shivered in disgust at the thought of these people and then ran away, jingling and squeaking, as quickly as their high-heeled shoes could carry them.

"Silly hens," said Gustav.

"Do you want something or not?" asked the skein of yarn through the window. She let out a little groan. "I'm about to go on break."

"Already?" asked Emma. "You just opened!"

The skein of yarn shrugged her shoulders.

"I'll have schnitzel," said Louise.

"Me too," said Gustav.

"There isn't any," said the skein of yarn. "I just have water and lettuce."

"How come?" asked Emma.

"Because models don't eat anything else," said the skein of yarn. "You saw that. Actually, I can even scrimp on the lettuce."

"But what smells so good here?" asked Gustav, sounding forlorn.

"My own food." The skein of yarn winked slyly and was just about to shut the window when Gustav cried: "Stop!" and shoved his fist in. "We're hungry!"

Emma had never seen him so angry.

"Pooh! That's what they all say. That doesn't matter," argued the skein of yarn.

Gustav shoved his face close to her. "Do you know that right here in this area there are two police officers running around? Very clever guys. They're looking for a nonbutton, one that's a child. Are you a child, perhaps?"

"Wh . . . What?" stammered the skein of yarn. "What kind of thing? I'm not a child. Whatever that is."

"Oh, really?" asked Gustav. "Should I just call the two police officers?"

"No! No!" shrieked the skein of yarn. "Fine. Here, have something!" She handed Gustav a plate.

"Schnitzel," he said, triumphantly. "I knew that's what I smelled."

Miffed, the skein of yarn slammed her window shut.

"Did you hear that?" asked Louise.

"What? That the skein of yarn didn't want to give us anything to eat?" Emma turned to Louise.

"No," she said dreamily. "The two models thought my hat was chic. They said I could get into the castle wearing it. That can mean only one thing, right?"

"This is delicious," grunted Gustav.

"No, not delicious," said Louise. Her eyes lit up. "It means that I'm valuable! Don't you agree?"

THE FAKE COWBOY

Emma, Louise, and Gustav wandered along the crocheted street for some time. Here and there were holes in the pattern, and they stumbled into them if they weren't paying attention. Emma got her shoe tangled up in a loose piece of wool and fell. It didn't hurt a bit, though; it was a little like slipping on a rug.

"Just keep going straight, that's what both of them said." Louise was full of energy since the models had praised her hat.

"Not so fast," gasped Gustav. "We don't have to rush that much."

"Oh, yes we do," retorted Louise. "Because it's almost afternoon, and we haven't met a single button since that silly snack bar. If we don't find a town or something by evening, we'll have to spend the night on this crocheted road, whether we want to or not."

Gustav made a long face, and Emma didn't have the slightest desire to spend the night on the street either, even if it did have such a pretty pattern. And besides, the crocheted road was coming to an end. Now, they were walking on sand; it was going uphill, and there were strange objects lining the street. Cacti? No, these were not real cacti; they were poison-green round pincushions with numerous pins stuck in them.

They nodded indifferently as Emma and her companions walked by.

"Ouch!" said Louise. She had accidentally stepped too close to a cactus pincushion.

"Just watch out," one of the needles piped up.

"Psst," whispered Gustav suddenly. "Do you hear that?"

They stopped and listened. It sounded like loud singing, very close by. Emma climbed onto a low velvety rock right in front of her and stuck out her head.

"There!" she shouted, surprised. She peered down into a little valley, where a group of brown metal buttons was sitting around a campfire. They were wearing fringed leather vests, cowboy hats, and boots with spurs.

"Play it again, Jesse," they bellowed, at which point one of the buttons blew into his harmonica and stamped his foot to the beat.

Old cowboy Jefferson,
on a ranch did dwell.
But he guzzled so much whiskey
that the ranch did not do well.
Hey, the ranch did not do well.

The metal buttons jumped up during the last line, danced bois-terously around the flickering fire, boxed with their fists in the air, and swung a lasso made of darning cotton. Nearby, a grasshopper grazed, wearing an embroidered saddle they had buckled onto him.

"What kind of characters are those?" asked Louise.

"Outlaws," murmured Gustav.

"You mean, they break the law?" asked Emma.

"Yes. Real Wild West guys." Feeling uneasy, Gustav watched the raucous mob. One of the buttons tripped while he was dancing and landed flat on his face. To Emma's surprise he broke out in tears.

"Sniveling sissy!" a half-rusted button yelled at him. "If you had blubbered like that panning for gold on the Klondike River, they'd have made mush out of you!"

"Plastic mush!" called another.

"Leave him alone. He was never a real cowboy." A copper button with a greenish face and a star embossed on his stomach waved his hand contemptuously. "He's never swung a real lasso. He was just on an imitation leather vest in the store! Humph! C'mon, go home to your girly-vest!" He laughed loudly, took the lasso from his hip, and flung it wildly in the air.

Emma, Louise, and Gustav watched the lasso fly by in amazement.

The fake cowboy button was still lying on the ground, sobbing loudly. ". . . Can't help it . . . on sale . . ."

Emma couldn't understand any more. She felt bad for the cowboy, even though she thought he could have shown a little more spunk.

"Another song!" somebody hollered.

But Jesse, who had the harmonica, had fallen asleep, and the others couldn't wake him up, no matter how much they jostled and tugged on him.

"Then Walter should sing a song," the star button decided.

With a malicious grin, he turned back to the poor fake cowboy button, who was crawling around on the ground looking for his glasses.

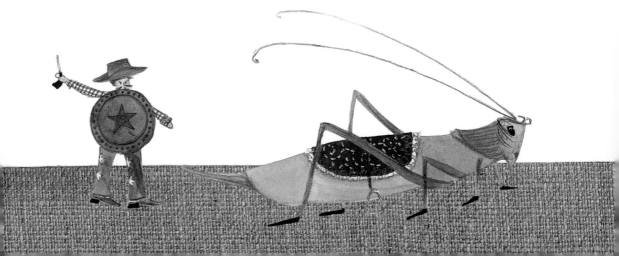

"I can't sing," he whimpered. "I can't do anything. I'm not even made out of metal, even if I look real, just plastic. It was a big sale, I . . ."

"Shut up!" barked the star button. "You sing something now. Move it!"

"Sh . . . Sh . . . She'll be coming 'round the mountain when she comes," croaked poor Walter desperately.

Emma couldn't stand it anymore. She jumped up and headed toward the cowboys.

"Don't!" squawked Gustav. "Have you gone crazy?"

"Hey, look," one of them said. The cowboy buttons gaped at Emma, who had appeared like a ghost from behind a cactus.

"What the heck is that?" whispered the star button. "An Indian?"

"I'm a child," Emma retorted rather sharply. "And you should be ashamed of yourselves for picking on Walter like that. If you want a song, then why don't you sing one yourselves?"

"Because we don't know any. We only know the song about old Cowboy Jefferson. Nothing else," said the star button, befuddled.

"And why not?" Emma put her hands on her hips. "Didn't you learn any songs in school?"

The buttons thought it over for a while. Walter stood up and knocked the dust from his pants.

"We never went to school," somebody answered at last. "We've always just been cowboys."

"Cowboys?" Emma looked at them skeptically.

"Gold Rush, California, 1849," said the star button with pride. "My owner was sheriff at first, and then the richest cowboy in the Wild West."

"I was there too," yelled the rusty one. "I was sewn on the first blue jeans. My sister was a cute little copper rivet; later, she emigrated to Colorado. Those were the days." He stared off at the sunset, a faraway look in his eyes. The others murmured their approval.

"And you never sang anything there?" asked Emma.

The buttons shook their heads. "We always drank so danged much whiskey. We can't remember anymore."

"Now," said Emma, more agreeable, "I can teach you a few songs. But first you have to promise me that you'll leave poor Walter in peace and not harm me or my friends."

"And how are we supposed to know that you won't turn us in to the police?" asked the star button.

"Because we are wanted by the police," said Gustav in a stern voice.

Unnoticed, he had come closer and was pulling the reluctant Louise by the arm behind. "We want to go to the lake and then to the castle."

"To the castle? What do you want there? That's where all those stuck-up jerks live," said Jesse, who had awakened in the meantime.

Walter nudged him. "There's a lady here, don't you see that?" He pointed at Louise, who was turning even redder than before.

"We just want to get there," retorted Gustav. That Constance was his reason was something he kept to himself. It didn't look like the cowboys understood much about love.

"A song." The husky request resounded from all sides. The grasshopper whinnied in alarm.

Emma sat down on the ground. "Well, all right," she began. "First, there's 'Aunt Lucky from Kentucky' and then 'Oh, Susanna' or even 'Oh My Darling, Clementine.'"

"Could you also sing 'Oh My Darling Constance'?" Gustav asked. Emma nodded.

Louise, in the meantime, had settled down next to Walter and was stroking his hand. "Don't worry about being made of plastic," she consoled him. "Maybe it will be a very valuable material someday. Who knows? The world changes so quickly." Then she joined Emma in the song; and after a while cheerful singing rang out from every mouth through the little valley.

The cowboys let Emma and her friends spend the night around their campfire, but, despite how tired Emma was, she couldn't fall asleep for some time. This was mainly because two cowboy buttons very near her were fighting about whether or not their lives had changed since the invention of the zipper. And furthermore, Louise chatted with Walter late into the night. The poor guy had suffered his whole life long, first from being poorly sewn onto a cheap imitation leather vest, and then from immediately falling off.

"Everything about me is shabby and unimportant," he whined in a low voice.

Louise, despite everything, found this preferable to her life as a spare button.

Emma gave a little sigh of frustration. The buttons' problems seemed ridiculously small compared to her own problem: Would she ever find her way back home?

Finally, she fell into an uneasy sleep.

NASTY MERMAIDS

The next day, the cowboys accompanied Emma, Louise, and Gustav to Western Town. It was teeming with wild metal buttons, all looking a bit ragged and unwashed. From a bar came the sounds of raucous caterwauling and laughing.

"This must be the town Mimi and Kitty mentioned. Where the people have such bad taste," murmured Gustav. He cast a sidelong glance at a stubbly-bearded silver rivet wearing dusty boots and a holey vest, who was lolling on a wooden bench in front of the saloon, smoking a pipe.

Somebody dumped a pail of water out a window onto a button who was walking by. In a flash, he picked up a rotten apple from the ground and threw it toward the window. Something clanked.

"I don't think the people here care at all if you're valuable or not," whispered Louise.

"Hey, look," shouted Emma, momentarily surprised.

The three friends could hardly believe their eyes. A little ahead of them were the paper clip and the coin from the hippie commune! They were fastening a sign over a store: Office and Sewing Supplies for the Modern Cowboy.

"Hello!" Emma called and waved at them.

"Well, what a coincidence," shouted the paper clip excitedly.

"So, you managed to escape too? You're safe from the police here; they never come to this town. My friend the coin and I have found a new home here. It doesn't matter to the cowboys if you're a button or not. We're just opening our store. Do you need anything?"

Emma turned to look at her friends. "I don't think so. We really just want to get to the castle."

The coin's eyes widened in horror. "To the castle? Why? There are so many police there! Better stay here. You could work in our store," he said, turning to Emma.

The paper clip nodded. "As a sales clerk. I take care of the ads, and the coin does the finances. What do you think?"

Emma felt her heart warm. What a friendly offer. But then she shook her head. "That's very kind, but I have to get back to my mother."

"Do you know how to get to the castle? Or at least to the lake?" Louise broke in impatiently. "If there's any way to do it, I'd like to get out of this town before sundown. I really don't like the way some people here are looking at my hat!"

In fact, quite a number of cowboy buttons had stopped, nudging their pals and pointing to the red stone.

The coin made an apologetic face. "I'm sorry; I have no idea where to find either the castle or the lake."

"But I do," came the sound of a shaking voice behind them.

They turned around and caught sight of Walter, the fake cowboy button, who was standing bashfully in front of the store. Hastily, he jumped to the side, just as a scuffed leather button came staggering by and almost knocked him over.

"Walter," said Louise happily.

"I kn . . . kn . . . know the way to the castle," said Walter, looking at his boots, which were made of plastic as well.

Louise twisted her hat back and forth coyly, until it almost fell off.

"Wonderful," said Emma. "Absolutely wonderful. Maybe you could come with us and show us the way?"

Walter was so happy that his plastic face cracked a little.

"There's nothing I would rather do," he said.

Following Walter, they waved to the coin and the paper clip one last time and trudged out of town single file along a road of tattered corduroy.

Emma thought about whether her aunt and uncle had noticed that she had disappeared. Would they look for her? Or, would her uncle simply be happy to have one less child to see? She banged into Gustav because Walter had come to a halt.

"There it is," he said solemnly and pointed downward. A glistening gray lake extended as far as the eye could see. Little waves rippled with a rustling sound onto a shore of thin, light green fabric.

Emma stuck her head out. It looked like a lake, and yet . . . .

She swiftly ran down to touch the water. Bewildered, she looked up.

"Silk," she said. "The lake is made of soft, cool, flowing silk! How can that be?"

"Yeah, well, what should it be made of?" asked Walter, astonished.

"Water," answered Emma. "Lakes are normally made of water."

"Water?" squealed Louise, shocked. "But that's not good for your skin at all! It'll make you rust!"

Emma hadn't even considered that. "Now, that may be—but how are you supposed to swim through silk? That's impossible."

Louise shrugged her shoulders. They all stared at the languid gray mass that fluttered softly back and forth in the wind.

"Could we run through it?" asked Gustav. "Hopefully we all have regular shoes on?"

Emma ran a few steps into the lake, but to her bewilderment, she sank in, just like in a lake made of water.

"I don't think this will work." Dejected, she looked around. "There!" she shouted in relief. "There's a boat!"

And, in fact, a short distance away there was a boat rocking in the silk sea. It was made from a half empty spool of thread. It was tied to a little pier and seemed to be asleep.

"Hurray!" Walter cried and jumped onto the pier in order to bring the boat in. Then he climbed in carefully.

"Watch out," droned the lethargic spool. "I'm not so young anymore. Do you have buttons with you? Otherwise I can't go."

"We do. Some very pretty ones, even." Walter looked over at Louise quickly.

Gustav, Emma, and Louise squeezed in, almost capsizing the tiny boat. But finally they managed to float out on the rippling waves.

"So, where's the island?" asked Louise. "I don't see anything."

"Do we have a compass?" asked Emma. She didn't exactly know how a compass could help them, but she knew that sailors in olden times had always managed with a compass.

"No. We'll find our way to the castle anyway," said Gustav, calming her.

"To the castle, to the castle, to the castle." The sudden singsong seemed to be coming from under the water.

Walter got so pale, that you could see through him. "Wh . . . what was that?" he whispered.

"What, what, what—you're getting a wet butt!" the voice sounded again. Somebody snickered.

And then their little boat began to rock.

"Hey! What's going on? Who's there? What are you doing here?" Emma cried, full of fear.

Only loud laughter, clear as a bell, sounded in answer. The boat was rocking so much now that Emma felt sick. They'd surely tip over soon.

"Stop!" Gustav roared. "Stop this instant!"

"Don't get all excited, old man!" A face popped up all of a sudden at the bow of the boat. A little figure pulled itself up effortlessly and sat down politely on the edge. The button had a wagging fish tail; she was fashioned top to bottom from a gorgeous iridescent material and had flame red hair, as well as numerous freckles. "We just want to have a little fun!"

"A little fun?" Gustav yelled in indignation. "A little fun? We're practically tipping over! And none of us can swim; we'll sink to the bottom right away!"

"Oops," said the iridescent button. "You can't swim?"

"I can," said Emma, "but not through silk."

"Neither can we," wailed Louise. "We're not fish, after all!"

Walter, feeling concern, nestled up against her.

"What do you mean by that, that I'm a fish?" The button with the fish tail narrowed her eyes. "I'm Albertine—a mermaid, you silly. Don't you see that I'm made of mother of pearl? We're all mermaids. And you're no fun at all. You can't take a joke." She twisted her mouth into a pout. Then she called down into the lake. "Keep it up. These guys are a drag."

Immediately the laughter and rocking started up again.

"Will you stop?" cried Gustav, now seriously worried,

Emma held on to the bow of the boat as though frozen. "Stop," she whispered. That's all she managed to utter.

"And one, and two," screeched the voices from the lake. Albertine gave a mischievous wave to Emma and her friends and slid back into the deep.

"And three," the mermaids shouted and laughed.

The boat tipped over. What had been on top was now on the bottom. Emma slid down and felt the cool layers of silk engulfing her, more and more. They lay on her, enfolded her, and took her breath away. It got harder and harder to stay on top, no matter how much she struggled.

"Help." Feebly she choked out the words. "Help!"

SAVIOR IN TIME OF DISTRESS

"Hold on tight! Hold on tight!"

The words reached Emma as though from a long distance. What was she supposed to hold on to? She was just about to sink to the bottom!

In front of her appeared a disc, which, on closer inspection, turned out to be Walter. He had lain on his back and was now floating flat on the surface of the lake. Since he was so light and made of plastic, he acted like a life preserver. Emma barely hesitated; she grabbed him with determination. Just then she saw that Louise and Gustav were holding fast to the other side of Walter's stomach.

"Is everything okay?" yelled Walter? "Are you all on?"

"Yes," Emma burst out. A red-haired head popped up right next to her and looked at her reproachfully. It was a mermaid, but not Albertine.

"You spoil sports!" grumbled the mermaid. "That was so much fun!"

Emma didn't answer. First of all, it seemed senseless trying to reason with this thing, and secondly, she just wanted to get out of the lake.

"Spoil sports! Spoil sports! Spoil sports!" chorused the other mermaids. They had all seated themselves on the overturned boat and were looking down at them. Their hair fluttered like red sails in the wind, and their mother of pearl glittered like silver in the sunshine.

Louise opened her mouth, but Emma beat her to it. "It doesn't make any difference if they're valuable or not. They're nasty and malicious."

Louise's mouth snapped shut. Giving in, she nodded.

Just then Gustav called, "Look!" He stuck out his arm and pointed to something far away on the horizon. Land! There was land in sight!

"The island," whispered Emma.

"About time," muttered Louise. "I won't be able hold on to my hat much longer."

Walter rowed a little with his left leg and set course for the island.

"See you later, wimps!" Albertine yelled down to them. "We'll wait here for you. You'll have to come back sometime!"

The others laughed spitefully; one did a triple flip into the water.

"Heck, no," murmured Gustav.

"I'd rather get melted down," said Walter.

Emma realized that she hadn't thanked him yet. "You saved us, Walter. Thank you very much!"

"Yes, Walter dear, that was awfully kind of you," Louise hurried to say, and Gustav nodded in agreement.

"No problem, no problem." Walter shrugged off the thanks. "At least I'm good for something."

"Now, don't be so hard on yourself," said Louise. "You are the most helpful and practical button I've ever met."

"Really?" stammered Walter. "You don't think I'm ridiculous?"

"Absolutely not."

"Thank you," said Walter, touched.

They floated on for a while in silence; the only sound for miles around was coming from the rippling silk when Walter spoke up again.

"Do you know, when I was young and inexperienced, I had no idea that I was only a fake cowboy button. I hung with the other buttons on the imitation leather vest in the store waiting for whatever was going to happen. We dreamed about the vastness of the prairie, campfires, and tough, adventuresome, courageous men we'd be with our whole life long . . . "

He cleared his throat. "And then this man with his hair parted on the side, wearing a suit, came into the store and asked for a vest he could wear to Mardi Gras. The sales clerk talked him into our vest, even though it was really tight over his stomach. The man griped a little about the price, which was already low, and took us home, where he put on a paper hat and buckled on a plastic gun. That really should have made us suspicious. But we were too excited. Then the man went into a bar full of people in strange clothes, running around, constantly flinging confetti over their heads, yelling, "Let the good times roll!" and drinking beer. It wasn't the way we'd pictured the Wild West at all. And in the end, I couldn't hold on against the pressure of his stomach—I burst off the vest, arched high in the air, and landed on the floor. Right away a high heel stepped on me, and the last thing I heard was "What an ugly, cheap costume Helmut's wearing. That vest is the most tasteless thing here tonight!"

Walter said nothing. Louise stroked him gently on the stomach.

"You're neither ugly nor cheap," Emma assured him. "You saved our lives."

Suddenly, there was a little jolt. They had arrived. The island stretched before them, and way up on top of a cliff loomed the majestic castle, which, Emma realized, was nothing more than a gigantic sewing basket with thousands of nested compartments.

AT THE TEA PARTY

A road of red velvet decorated with a gold border led to the castle.

"How comfortable it is to walk on this," Gustav sighed with happiness. "And maybe my dearest Constance goes up and down here several times a day. Just the thought of it makes me happy."

Louise had become very quiet; she just adjusted her hat over and over.

Even Emma was lost in thought. What should they actually say when they got to the castle? And what if the people in the castle didn't hear them out, but instead locked them up right away? A cold shiver ran down her back as she thought of Isolde's stuck-up face.

"What are we actually going to tell them?" Louise asked. She seemed to be able to read minds. "And what if they won't even let Emma in? After all, she's not a button."

"Time will tell," said Walter nervously.

Then the entrance to the castle appeared before them—a big wooden gate guarded by two safety pins. When they noticed the little group, they leaned against each other and blocked the entrance.

"Who are you?" they rasped in unison. "And what do you want here?"

Gustav extended his hand, which the two guards totally ignored. "Gustav is my name. I'm looking for my fiancée, an exquisitely carved button who was attached to the same traditional costume I was. Her name is Constance."

The right safety pin squinted at him nearsightedly and then consulted in a whisper with his colleague. The second one scrutinized Gustav and said, "We don't know Constance, so she can't be here. She's probably even prohibited."

"Nonsense," Gustav objected, outraged. "How can she be prohibited?"

"All unknown things are prohibited," explained the right safety pin. "And because we don't know Constance, logically, she's prohibited."

"That thing there is also prohibited," said the left guard, pointing to Emma.

"Exactly. We're not familiar with it. It's prohibited," the right one agreed.

"Maybe it's even a Constance," the left one commented slyly. Both grinned. "A Constance and unfamiliar. Doubly prohibited."

"What?" asked Gustav, confused.

Emma was getting really furious. "My name isn't Constance; it's Emma, and I want to see Lady Isolde," she explained in her sternest voice. The kind of voice her mother used when she wanted Emma to clean up her room.

The safety pins remained completely unimpressed. "You're prohibited, Constance," said the left one, leaning on his long pointy leg. "You can't get through here."

"But I," said Louise, making herself noticeable, "but I can get through." She shoved her way in front of Emma and stood right in the sun, so that the red stone in her hat lit up like a glowing ball.

"My goodness," said the left safety pin. "Why didn't you tell us right away that you had somebody aristocratic with you? Come right in, come right in!" They snapped closed quickly and let Louise through. As Emma was about to slip in right behind her, they blocked the way again.

"Not you," spat the right safety pin. "Not the other two either. The castle isn't for common people."

Louise turned around and walked back. "Either all or none," she said. "You don't want to argue with me, do you? After all, I could be extremely valuable."

"But that's impossible," moaned the right safety pin and bit his wire lip all crooked. "I'm not allowed. I'm not allowed to let them in."

"Of course you are," retorted Louise. "After all, these are my servants."

"What?" Gustav said indignantly, but Emma gave him a quick shove in the ribs.

"Yes, that's true," said Walter. "We worship her." He looked at Louise with a flaming expression in his eyes.

"Well, if that's the case . . . " The two guards shrugged their shoulders and cleared the way. Emma hurried to get through before they changed their minds. But the two had found a new topic already.

"She had three servants; did you see that?" Emma heard one of them say. "And people like us have to do everything ourselves. How is that fair, I ask you?"

"Tell me about it," the other one agreed. "Someday, I'm going to shove this job and get out of here. After all, there are jobs in security all over the place."

Emma wasn't listening anymore. She was too excited. Now they were going step-by-step up into the castle. The walls were hung and decorated with the finest embroidered tapestries. Tied-back draperies fluttered in place of doors, and all around a humming bustle prevailed. Nobody seemed to notice them. Emma saw elegant buttons with carvings or ornate patterns scampering on their tiny shoes through the corridors, little pins with small, colorful heads who were apparently working as chambermaids and racing right by them, and portly stag horn buttons strutting around with an air of importance, carrying some sort of documents.

"Excuse me." Gustav tried to get their attention, but nobody stopped.

"Pardon me," Walter whispered now too, but nobody heard his timid voice.

"Louise, where are you going?" asked Emma, because Louise was running purposefully from one corridor to another.

"I don't know," she answered. "I'm simply following those really chic buttons."

And sure enough—all the elegant buttons seemed to be running in one direction. But where were they going? Finally, Emma couldn't stand it anymore. She stepped right in the path of a little pink-headed pin, who fell over, startled, with a clank.

"Excuse me, most gracious one," whispered the little pin, who just wanted to run along.

"Now stay still," said Emma, holding her with a firm grip. She could feel how the poor thing was trembling with fright. "Where are all the buttons running off to?"

"To the tea party," whispered the little pin. "To Lady Wedgwood's tea party."

"Lady Wedgwood?" Gustav frowned. "Might a certain lady by the name of Isolde also be there?"

"Lady Isolde?" squeaked the little pin, now terrified. "I hope not . . . I mean . . . " Her little pink head turned bright red. "Of course, I really hope that the charming Lady Isolde will be there," she finished, glancing around nervously.

"How do we get there?" asked Emma, without letting go of the little pin, no matter how much the pin pulled and tugged.

"I . . . I'm going there too," she finally admitted in anguish. "I was told to bring new tablecloths." She nodded at the big pile of sparkling white tablecloths she had almost dropped when she fell.

"Oh," said Emma, and let go of the little pin, who galloped off at once like a runaway horse.

"After her!" shouted Gustav.

93

The friends lost no time and chased after the little pin, who was fleeing in panic, through the corridors and archways, up and down stairs, and finally into a big room. A vast number of blue and white button ladies, most of them decorated with artistic reliefs, were gathered there. The light blue walls of the room were adorned with silhouettes, and many of the button ladies held delicate blue cups in their hands, with their pinky fingers elegantly in the air.

The little pin threw the tablecloths into a basket and ran straight out of the room again. Emma and her friends stopped and gasped for breath. After a couple of seconds, they noticed that the whole room had fallen silent, and all eyes were on them. Eyes full of horror, unease, and shock.

And then someone broke away from the tea-drinking crowd.

It was a big round golden button lady at whom Emma stared open-mouthed. Isolde herself.

"I don't believe it," she said, opening her golden eyes as wide as plates. "You rude thing, following me even to my own tea party! I reported you; why haven't those idiot police officers locked you up yet? Or, do you want to turn yourself in as a nonbutton? Turn herself in, isn't that funny, ladies?" Isolde looked around, seeking approval; and sure enough, several of those present let out a frightened giggle.

"Is that one really made out of plastic?" whispered a blue lady in a white wig, pointing at Walter. Her neighbor nodded and dropped her cup in fright.

"Take them away," bellowed Isolde. "Take them away, the whole lot. What kind of impudence, not only not being a button, but also disrupting our tea party!"

But just at that moment Louise stepped forward and said, "No!"

A murmur went through the crowd.

LOUISE'S FATE

The way Louise was standing there, her little chin sticking out provocatively and the heavy hat on her head, with the red stone now seeming to shine twice as brightly in the center—that was really an impressive sight.

"Enchanting, quite enchanting," said one of the blue ladies.

The other ladies whispered among themselves; one even stepped forward and took a monocle out of her purse in order to get a better look at Louise.

"Who are you?" asked Isolde. She scrutinized Louise with a mixture of distrust and envy.

"Louise is my name," said Louise.

"Your hat, is that . . . is that by any chance . . . ?" Isolde eyed the red stone, full of desire, but didn't dare to express what she was thinking.

"It looks like a semi-precious stone," came a voice from the tea party, where a number of ladies were now having an intense discussion.

"What are they talking about?" Emma asked Gustav in a hushed voice. Isolde seemed to have forgotten all about them.

"Is a semi-precious stone valuable?" asked Louise, breathless.

The light blue ladies exchanged amused glances. Finally, one came forward from the crowd. "My dear, half of these ladies here would happily let the holes in their middles get walled up to be as valuable

as a semi-precious stone." She smiled at Louise and held out her hand. Louise turned hesitantly toward Emma, Gustav, and Walter and then took a step toward the ladies.

"Oh my goodness!" shrieked one all of a sudden. She had already turned dark blue from envy. "That's not a semi-precious stone!"

"Not a semi-precious stone?" The ladies' whispered, gossip grew louder, Isolde grinned in elation.

"No, no, not what you're thinking!" The dark blue lady, overwhelmed with excitement, fanned herself so that she wouldn't faint. "That's a gemstone!"

There was a sudden commotion. If the ladies had held off up to now, they no longer showed any restraint and pounced on Louise, anxious to talk to her, shake her hand, serve her a little cup of tea, or even—if they were extremely lucky—to touch the bright red gemstone.

With her last ounce of strength, the lady holding the fan gasped, "A ruby." Then she had to sit down for the time being.

"Very beautiful, very beautiful, I am so exceedingly happy for you, my dear," said Isolde to Louise. Her face, however, expressed just the opposite. "Of course, you are extremely welcome here among us, dearest Louise; drink a little cup of tea with us, eat a little pastry." Isolde turned around, searching. "Lady Wedgwood?" she yelled across the room. "Where did the worthless servants get off to with the pastries?"

Lady Wedgwood was nowhere to be seen; at the very least she wasn't making herself noticeable. Instead, Isolde's eyes fell on Emma, and a cunning look came over her face. "Now, as far as these three go, we are hardly dealing with gemstones, semi-precious or precious. Or industrial grade," she added and let out a whinnying laugh. Then she got serious again. "The nonbutton by the name of child will be taken away, the pathetic plastic-face can work as a stable boy as far as I'm concerned, and the other one can be a servant, for all I care." She clapped her hands. "Come on, get moving. Where is a safety pin when you need one?"

Emma began to tremble from fear and indignation. Nevertheless, she tried to make her voice steady. "Your dearest ladyship Isolde, I need your help," she said loudly and hoped that this time Isolde would notice how polite Emma was. "I just need to touch you quickly; then I can get back to where I came from. That would be okay, right?"

"Touch me?" Isolde uttered a squeaky noise and jumped back, horrified. "Touch me? That's the last thing I need! Then anybody could come up to me. I'm aristocratic! And you're nothing; you're not even a button! Servants!" she yelled, beside herself with indignation. "Where's that riffraff off to now?"

"Please." Now Gustav, too, came to Emma's defense. "It will just take a moment, and while we're at it, maybe we could inquire if

there is somebody here by the name of Constance? A ravishingly beautiful button from a traditional costume with a splendid singing voice, whom I—"

"Everybody shut up!" screamed Isolde. "What were you thinking?"

"What was he thinking? I'll be glad to explain." All of a sudden Louise tore herself away from her admirers, her lips narrowed in fury. "He would like to find Constance, because he loves her more than anything else in the world. Even though I don't believe that you, Isolde, understand what love is. And Gustav may be just a simple carved button, but he accompanied us this far, and he's my friend. And as far as Emma is concerned," here Louise's voice got even louder, so loud that all the other conversations stopped, "without Emma's help I would never have made it to the castle and would never have found out how valuable I am."

"But," sputtered Isolde. However, Louise didn't let her finish speaking.

"Am I more valuable than you, dear Isolde? I think so. So, keep your mouth shut!"

Isolde kept silent, offended.

"And then there's Walter—a simple plastic button, that may well be. But behind this plastic chest beats a heart of gold! Walter saved us all!" Louise was now standing in the middle of the room; sunlight shone through an open window and was refracting in Louise's ruby, making a captivating display.

"If I've learned anything on our trip, it's this: It doesn't matter at all if a button is made out of plastic or a gemstone. No, it doesn't even matter if somebody's a button or a paperclip or a child. Whatever that is," she added. "What is important is what a person does."

Emma thought that Louise had never looked prettier. A few ladies applauded, slightly confused, but stopped suddenly because at that moment, something extraordinary happened. It got dark. Something had blocked out the sun.

The little pin with the pink head appeared in the doorway, white as chalk, and tried to say something, but all she could get out was "M . . . M . . . M . . ."

"Speak properly, pin, what's the matter?" asked one of the blue ladies impatiently.

At that moment Emma felt a gust of wind so strong, it seemed as though a helicopter was going to land next to her. Something appeared at the window, a horrible, ghastly, black something, something that made all the buttons cry out in panic. Glass tinkled, and something gigantic zoomed at breakneck speed through the air, black and menacing. It set its course for Louise, plunged downward, rose again like an arrow, and flew off. The sun returned as suddenly as it had disappeared. The spot where Louise had been standing was empty.

"M . . . Magpie approaching," said the little pin.

THE VELCRO HOLDS IT CLOSED! HURRAY!

"Louise?" Emma couldn't believe what had just happened. Walter, who was standing next to her, started sobbing horribly, and Gustav had turned snow-white from fear. Everyone in the room was paralyzed. Except Isolde.

"Pride goes before a fall; such is the case here," Isolde remarked, impassive. "How she just had to show off that hat. Every button knows that magpies are attracted by that kind of sparkle."

"But we have to help her!" Emma exclaimed.

Isolde looked her over coolly. "I can hardly believe that I'm still carrying on a conversation with an impudent thing like you; even so, you should know that we don't have to do anything. Everyone is responsible for himself."

"And how should we help her, anyway?" mentioned a lady whose wig was somewhat tattered from the shock. "Perhaps we should fight this monstrous magpie? That's totally impossible."

"But," Emma stammered. "But . . . "

She thought about it for a second.

"Of course we can help her! By touching Isolde, I'll get big again and I'll be able to free Louise."

"Don't you even dare try to touch me!" screamed Isolde.

Emma could hear Gustav huffing.

His face had the same angry look that Emma had seen at Yarny's Snack Bar.

"If you don't let this child touch you this minute, you won't know what hit you!" he shouted. "It makes no difference to me how golden or valuable you are. Don't you have a heart?"

"No," responded Isolde flippantly. "What for?"

"Please." Emma tried one last time. She was totally desperate. "You know, in my aunt's house, I saved you from the cat; don't you remember that?"

"I hate cats," said Isolde. "Even more than magpies." With that, she turned around but jerked to a stop. A frightened whispering went through the room. It grew dark again outside the window!

"The magpie's coming back!" somebody screamed.

"Help," shrieked a woman's high voice, and everyone dashed to the door. But it was too late. The last windowpanes broke with a tinkling sound, and something big and black squeezed into the room from outside.

All the buttons screamed their heads off; Emma, however, couldn't believe her eyes. Was it possible? "Victor!" she shouted in amazement. "Is it really you?"

"Of course it is!" he exclaimed jauntily and unfolded himself so that he reached up to the ceiling and towered over all the buttons. "I thought I would accept Emma's offer to look for my poets' quartet.

Writing poetry alone isn't any fun. So I followed you. And the way it looks, I got here just at the right time, didn't I?"

Emma laughed in relief, while the ladies anxiously squeezed up against the wall.

"You know the monster?" whispered Walter.

"Victor," shouted Gustav. "You have to help us again. Hold on tight to the golden lady there." He pointed to Isolde, who was scurrying on her little legs through the room toward the door.

Victor simply folded out his right side and blocked her way.

"What are you thinking? Let me go!" screamed Isolde.

Emma, who now understood what Gustav was planning, began to run. "Hold her tight, Victor, hold her tight!" she shouted.

"That's outrageous! Help! I'll report you all! Ow! My hairdo! Let me go! I'm an aristocrat!" Isolde struggled like a madwoman and got more and more entangled in Victor's bristles.

Now Emma was standing right in front of her. She reached out her hand and said, "Aristocratic or not—you're the nastiest button in the world." Then she tapped Isolde's cold cheek with her finger.

"Be polite!" shrieked Isolde. "Your ladyship, you are the nastiest . . . "

Emma didn't hear the rest.

Without warning it got dark.

EMMA'S WISHES

When it got light again, Emma was lying on the floor of the button room. The window was wide open, as was the door to the hall. Emma stood up and teetered a little. How strange it was to be suddenly big again and to be standing on a wooden floor. She looked around. There they were—all the buttons, in their cartons and boxes and hiding places. Where were Gustav, Walter, and Victor? And where was Louise? The magpie. Emma ran to the window and looked out. In the cherry tree in the yard, a black-and-white bird was raising a racket. She flapped her wings hysterically as she noticed Emma, who climbed right out the window, since it was the easiest thing to do, and made her way hand over hand along a gnarly overhanging branch. Hopefully it wouldn't break off. And hopefully Louise was still with the magpie.

Carefully, Emma climbed higher. The magpie ranted and raved, but didn't move from the spot. Maybe she had eggs in her nest? Puffing and panting, Emma worked herself up to the same height as the magpie.

"Where did you drag Louise off to, you thieving bird?" she murmured.

The magpie looked at her out of black, button-like eyes and flew a bit higher. Farther up in the tree Emma spotted a round thing made of dry sticks. She climbed some more, slipped, gave a little cry, and pulled herself up again. There! There was the nest. And in the middle—between a broken piece of a mirror and a silver ring, which surely belonged to Aunt Mechthild—lay a little silver button with a lovely red stone in the middle.

"Louise, my dear," Emma whispered and took the button out.

High up in the sky, the magpie was almost going berserk with rage. But Emma didn't care. She was as big as a normal girl again—what could a ridiculous magpie do to her?

"Shoo, shoo!" said Emma. "Get lost! And don't ever swipe another button!"

The magpie squawked in a huff and flew away.

Carefully, Emma put the Louise button in her skirt pocket and started back down. At that moment there was a piercing scream.

"Emma! For heaven's sake, Emma! There she is. I found her, Hubie; she's in the tree."

A completely distraught Aunt Mechthild appeared under the tree. Over and over again she clapped her hands in surprise and from time to time she rubbed her eyes, as if she couldn't believe what she was seeing. "You're in the tree? Were you there the whole time? Why? We looked for you all over the place!"

"You looked for me?" asked Emma, dumbfounded. She held on tight to the trunk and stood on the last branch.

"But of course, my child, we were really worried about you!" Uncle Hubert came at a run; his cardigan fluttered like a flying carpet behind him. As he was running, his dentures fell out; he picked them up without stopping and crammed them back into his mouth without giving it a second thought. "Thank God!" he gasped, "Thank God."

Emma was completely speechless. Her aunt and uncle were seriously worried about her?

"How long was I gone?" she asked cautiously.

"Eight hours. Eight whole hours," shouted her aunt.

"We didn't do any more puzzles for the rest of the day, we were so upset. And your mother's coming to get you the day after tomorrow; she called a little while ago!"

Emma's mother was finally coming to get her? And the other two hadn't worked on their puzzle anymore? They must have been really frightened. But how could Emma have been gone only eight hours? Maybe time went faster in Buttonland? She slid down from the branch and in no time found herself pressed into Aunt Mechthild's ample bosom.

"Didn't you like it at our house? Tell me, where were you all that time?"

Emma could feel the Louise button in her pocket; she heard the magpie making a racket in the distance and saw the open window to the button room behind her uncle. She thought about Gustav, about Walter, the paper clip, and the coin, about Victor and Isolde and the lake made out of suffocating silk. How was she ever supposed to explain that to anybody? Her aunt and uncle looked at her expectantly. They must have just jumped up from supper, because there was a little piece of egg yolk stuck to Uncle Hubert's cardigan. Who would believe her?

So all she said was, "In the tree. I was in the tree the whole time. I was asleep."

Her aunt and uncle exchanged a worried look.

"Are you all right now?" asked her uncle. "Do you need anything? Can we get you a treat? Maybe a pu—"

He didn't get any farther. Aunt Mechthild stomped on his foot so that he grimaced in pain. "Pudding," he said with a strained smile. "Maybe some of Mrs. Schulz's pudding?"

Emma thought it over for a moment.

"I don't want any pudding," she said.

Aunt Mechthild's cautious smile faded. "What do you want then my dear child?"

"A puz––" Uncle Hubert spoke up once again, but this time Aunt Mechthild stomped on him so hard that he howled.

"I want something else," Emma declared.

"Sure, sure, whatever you want," Aunt Mechthild was quick to say. "A roll? Some cocoa? A warm bath?"

107

Emma shook her head. "I want three things," she said. "First of all, I want you to get me three Velcro fasteners."

"What?" asked her aunt.

"You mean—buy new ones?" her uncle asked, dismayed.

"They don't have to be new." Emma thought about it briefly. "Just the opposite; the older, the better."

"And secondly?" asked her aunt.

"Secondly, I would like to straighten up the button room. Alone," Emma added, when she noticed her aunt's horrified look.

"The button room?" Aunt Mechthild turned white as chalk. "What do you want in there? It's dangerous there; I . . . " She stopped talking suddenly and bit her lip. At that moment, something incredible occurred to Emma. Her aunt's red hair was so crinkly and straggly; it hung on her head like . . . wool! The paper clip's words came to mind. Could it be that her aunt had once been to Buttonland herself but didn't want to admit it? And maybe that's why she was afraid to go into the room?

Curtly, Emma answered, "I have something to take care of in there." Her aunt shivered, as if she was having an eerie memory, but then she nodded.

"And thirdly?" asked her uncle.

He hadn't noticed Aunt Mechthild's distress. Apparently, he was just relieved that none of the wishes would plunge him into ruin.

"And thirdly, I would like you two to buy me a pair of lederhosen."

"Lederhosen," her aunt repeated mechanically. "Of course." Her tone of voice was full of exaggerated patience; it was the one she normally reserved for small children, the critically ill, and observations about Uncle Hubert's teeth falling out.

"Not just any lederhosen," said Emma. "But a used pair of men's lederhosen, one with a button missing from the left suspender."

"Used and missing a button. That's not expensive," said her uncle happily. "That's easy to arrange." He scratched his head. "We might possibly even have something like that in the house. Then we wouldn't have to spend any money. What do you think, my dear?"

Her aunt furrowed her brow. "Of course, we'll look around in the house first!" she shouted at Uncle Hubert. "Since when do we throw money out the window?"

"And before I straighten up the button room, I would like some cocoa," said Emma.

"Whatever you want, sweetie," Aunt Mechthild hastily promised.

"Yes, that's what I want," said Emma. Then she went into the house.

There was no time to lose.

EMMA STRAIGHTENS UP

Being big again was strange. Yet, that's all Emma had wished for the whole time she was little. She missed Gustav, Walter, and Louise. Again and again she took the silver and red button out of her pocket and stroked it gently with her finger. What was Louise thinking, lying there in Emma's hand? At least they had found out that Louise was worth a great deal. Emma would take care of everything else as soon as possible. For the time being she would just eat supper as usual.

With a loud groan, Mrs. Schulz had brought a tray with sandwiches and an egg and had complained to Uncle Hubert about a woman of her age having to be on the go all day long. Even so, she seemed to be glad that Emma was there again, because she could show Emma the new varicose vein in her leg. "Comes from standing so much," she had boasted. Then she had flounced off.

Uncle Hubert was sitting next to Emma, sighing sorrowfully every now and then. Emma could just imagine what was wrong with him. He had begun to put the pieces of eggshell together again in order to reproduce the original egg. An egg puzzle.

"Aunt Mechthild will be back soon." He'd been saying that over and over again for more than an hour. Her aunt had dashed off right away to fulfill Emma's wishes. Every once in a while Emma could hear a loud clanking or clattering in the house. Apparently, her aunt was rummaging through every drawer and box. And it seemed both of them had a very guilty conscience. When Emma was full and went to the button room, her uncle padded unhappily behind her. Emma stopped.

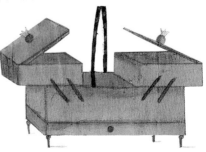

"I'm doing this alone," she said, her voice pleasant.

"But don't throw anything out," her uncle requested with an anxious look.

"I won't toss anything out. I'm just tidying up."

Her uncle still didn't leave. He must have gotten instructions from her aunt to watch over Emma so she didn't disappear again all of a sudden.

110 "Why don't you do a nice little puzzle?" asked Emma.

Uncle Hubert could hardly believe his good luck. "You wouldn't mind?" he stammered.

"No, as long as it's only a little one."

"A tiny little one," her uncle exclaimed with joy. "The tiniest, littlest, itty bitty puzzle in the world! It's . . . " he said and faltered. Evidently it was taking a great deal of effort for him to say this. He started again. "It's nice . . . nice to see you, Emma." Then he bolted.

Emma took a deep breath and made her way into the button room. Where should she start? The castle. She had to find the sewing basket with the nested compartments.

After she had looked for a while in countless boxes full of buttons, all of a sudden she noticed something that looked familiar. A pile of glossy gray fabric lay carelessly discarded on the floor. Silky gray fabric . . . the lake! It was the lake! She dug her finger in and fished two little mother of pearl buttons out of the depths of the fabric. "You nasty little meanies!" she murmured. Then she threw them back indifferently because she had found what she was looking for: the open sewing basket. And right in front of it lay two safety pins! Emma took a quick look through all the little compartments. They were lined with red velvet—and in the biggest

compartment was an accumulation of blue and white buttons. Right at the edge was a carved button from a traditional costume and a nondescript plastic button. Gently, Emma lifted them both up and put them in her pocket with Louise. Was she imagining it, or did she hear soft cheering?

Emma smiled. But she still wasn't finished. With spiteful fingers she tried to grab the big round gold button in the middle of the compartment. But it rolled away suddenly. She stuck her hand out again, but then stopped, alarmed. What if touching Isolde made her shrink again? Hesitantly, she looked around. The first time the door to the hall had been closed. Now it was wide open. It simply had to work. "You stay here, you meanie," Emma murmured. She took a deep breath and snatched the big round thing. Nothing happened. She breathed out in relief and stuck Isolde in her other skirt pocket. There was also a little piece of Velcro neatly folded together in the corner of the compartment. "Victor, you're not all that big," Emma whispered. She stuck him in with Gustav, Walter, and Louise.

Then she meandered through the room. She found a box full of junk in which a long wooden button was lying close beside a faded white satin button. Woody and Miranda. She took them both along, as well as the marker cap, the stones, and the snail shell. She would put those things back in the right rooms afterward. The skein of yarn she left behind, as well as the glittering Chanel buttons, which she found in a gold bowl. Just as she found a pile of rusty metal buttons in a particularly dusty corner of the room, her aunt came in with Emma's sheepish uncle in tow, looking in from behind.

"Well, have you found something beautiful?" she inquired with a strained smile. Emma nodded.

"Oh, a coin!" shouted her aunt, who, suddenly delighted, wanted to pick up the coin, which was lying next to a paper clip near the rusty buttons.

"No!" Emma shouted. "Leave it alone."

"Why?" Aunt Mechthild looked at her in amazement.

"Because . . . " Emma gulped. "Because the coin has to stay there. He's happy there."

Aunt Mechthild cast Uncle Hubert a meaningful glance. Emma probably hit her head somehow, but whatever that strange child did in the tree for eight hours cannot ever become public, is what that look meant.

"Of course, the coin may stay there, if that's what you'd really like," she said. She rummaged in her jacket pocket and pulled something out. "Here. Three Velcro fasteners, just like you wanted. Lying in the drawer with all the other handy things that can always be reused."

Emma grabbed them and pulled Victor out of her pocket to compare him. He was an exact match!

"Well, well," said her astonished uncle. "Where did you get the fourth one? Do they belong together?"

"Yes. They're a quartet," whispered Emma.

"And then there's this," said her aunt. With mild disgust she handed Emma a rather tattered pair of lederhosen. "I certainly don't know what you want with this old thing, but at least we don't have to buy one. These were with Uncle Hubert's emergency clothes on the third floor."

"So, there was something good there?" Her uncle was astonished. "I had no idea that I owned such a nice pair of pants."

And while he and her aunt argued quietly over whether or not he was still allowed to wear the pants, Emma grabbed them eagerly. They smelled a little musty, like moth spray and a closet full of clothes; the side seam was ripped, and the seat was worn through—but the suspenders were still intact. The left side was empty, but on the right side was a pretty carved button. It was hanging by just a thread. Constance.

"Gustav," whispered Emma gently, "I hope the joy of seeing her again doesn't leave you speechless!" And with a firm tug she pulled Constance off the suspender and shoved her into her pocket next to Gustav.

"My beautiful pants," her uncle moaned under his breath.

"Are you satisfied now, my dear?" asked her aunt. She jabbered on and on at Emma without taking a breath. "It's nice at our house, isn't it, my child? You shouldn't hide in the tree, we love you more than anything, don't forget to tell your mother how nice we've been to you, you hear—"

"Aunt Mechthild," Emma cut her off. "Can you show me how to sew?" A wonderful idea had just come to her.

"Sew?" asked her aunt, thrown for a loop. "Depends on what it is. What do you want to sew?"

"A collar and a skirt," said Emma.

FRIENDS

Two days later, Emma waved to her uncle and aunt one last time. They stood in front of their big house looking infinitely relieved. Next to them on the ground sat Pepper the cat. He kept jerking his head back and forth in order to look at his new collar. It was obvious that he was especially interested in the big, round gold button which was finally his, and which Emma, with Aunt Mechthild's guidance, had sewn on firmly.

"Have fun, Isolde," murmured Emma.

"What did you say, my precious darling?" asked her mother. She was sitting next to Emma in the car, steering through the big gate.

"Nothing."

"I'm so glad that I was able to come get you earlier. Were you really bored there? There isn't really much for children to do at Uncle Hubert and Aunt Mechthild's. And all that junk that the two of them collect . . . " She shook her head in bewilderment. "Oh well, it doesn't surprise me. From what I've heard, Uncle Hubert was strange, even as a child."

"Did he keep everything he found back then?" asked Emma.

Her mother nodded, amused. "And how. You know—he's really Granny's brother. You just call him uncle. And she told me that, as a child, he got a new room every year because he hoarded so many treasures that the old one got too little."

"And was he a jigsaw puzzle fanatic then too?"

Emma couldn't for the life of her imagine Uncle Hubert as a little boy. With his own teeth!

"No," answered her mother. "Aunt Mechthild brought the puzzle obsession into the marriage." She thought for a minute. "But not at the beginning, really. Not until she'd had a little nervous breakdown. Right before the wedding to Uncle Hubert."

"Was she afraid that he would run away with a fat woman from the bowling club?" asked Emma, startled. Miranda's sad story came right to mind.

"Of course not! What strange ideas you come up with!" Emma's mother shook her head in surprise. "No, nobody knows exactly what was wrong with her. One evening she disappeared somewhere in the house for several hours; no one could find her."

"And then?" Emma asked with bated breath.

"Then, all of a sudden, she turned up, completely hysterical, saying incoherent stuff about some commune and that they wanted to arrest her and that she wasn't a button. Completely nuts." Emma's mother braked sharply as they turned the corner. Then she continued. "Uncle Hubert gave her a puzzle then to calm her down; she sat in front of it for hours, pushing one piece into another. After that, she was normal—well, as far as you can call Aunt Mechthild normal." Emma's mother giggled. "From that day on she was a puzzle fanatic."

Emma tugged excitedly at her sleeve. "Did she . . . did she ever say anything about the commune?"

Her mother frowned.

"No, I can't remember. I think she just had a funny dream. From that day on, the only thing she's collected like crazy is buttons." She glanced over at Emma. "Well, at least she taught you how to sew, right?"

"Yes," said Emma. "And I even found a few friends."

"Oh, really?" Her mother was surprised.

Emma rubbed her little finger over her new skirt. There she had personally sewn a cheerful border—consisting of two carved buttons very much in love, an unbelievably valuable ruby button, an unusually handy plastic button, a wooden hippie button who was snuggled up to his new bride, Miranda, as well as a literary quartet.

"Really," said Emma.

ULRIKE RYLANCE, was born in Jena in 1968. She studied both English and German languages and literature in Leipzig and London. After completing her studies, she worked in London for ten years teaching German to children and adults. Since 2001, she has lived in Seattle with her husband and two daughters, writing books for children and young adults. Her first young adult novel, *Ein Date für vier* (*A Date for Four*), was published in 2010.

Library of Congress Cataloging-in-Publication Data is available on file.
ISBN: 978-1-62087-992-4

Manufactured in China, May 2013
This product conforms to CPSIA 2008

SILKE LEFFLER, who was born in Vorarlberg in 1970, first completed an apprenticeship as a dressmaker and then studied textile design. Since 1996 she has worked as a freelance textile designer for prestigious international firms. She has also been working as a children's book illustrator and designer of stationary products since 1998. She lives with her family in southern Germany.